Our Sweet Romance Series

Love's Way Back

Laura HERVEY

Alabaster Box Press

Text copyright © 2020 by Laura Hervey
Alabaster Box Press
Akron, New York

Cover design and title page designed by
Paper and Sage Design

ISBN Trade 978-1-7325187-4-2
ISBN POD 978-1-7325187-3-5
ISBN e-book 978-1-7325187-2-8
Library of Congress Control Number: 2020919283
Printed in the United States of America

Dedication

To every person who has ever struggled
to find their way back.

Acknowledgements

Without the expertise and encouragement of my faithful critique partners, Gloria Clover, Linda Turner, and Carol Hamilton, this book might never have been completed. To both, I owe a debt of gratitude. Special thanks go to my four beta readers, Jeanne Fuller, Sarah Rizzo, Mary Duggan, and Pat Means. Finally, for her assistance in understanding the methods of a canine behavioral specialist, I thank Sarah Dolph Hogg. Any errors regarding dog training are mine, not hers.

Chapter One

Determined not to cry, Julie Barnes swallowed hard, but the tight panic in her chest escalated. Tears changed nothing. Tears were counterproductive and would put her at a disadvantage with the real estate agent. Still, Julie couldn't keep her gaze from scanning Shady Meadows' panoramic view. The fifty-acre farm had belonged to Aunt Elaine and Uncle Fred, and now, it was Julie's. From the white clapboard farmhouse with its wraparound porch to the expansive fields beyond the barns, every square foot of the farm was precious to Julie. But it was the horses grazing in the pasture that caused two rebellious tears to trickle down her cheeks. She and her brother, Jack, had spent many hours horseback riding with Uncle Fred on the winding trails through the woods. But now was not the time to be sentimental. **Selling Shady Meadows was best for** everyone. Julie brushed away all evidence of her lapse in control.

The real estate agent patted Julie's arm. "Are you all right, dear? It can be extremely hard losing someone you love. Being in their home brings back so many memories."

Unable to handle compassion from a stranger, Julie faced the stylish woman in her sleek navy suit. "Please let's just focus on why you're here."

Frustration flashed across the realtor's face, but Ms. Morrison quickly composed her features into a soothing but professional expression. "Perhaps, you'd like to wait a few weeks before putting this on the market."

Did she want to wait? What difference would waiting make? Julie would still feel obligated to sell. Splitting the profit with her parents and her brother was the only fair thing to do. Wasn't it?

But having her own space at last—after choosing to postpone living in her own apartment to buy the building that now housed Julie's Canine Jewels—would be beyond awesome. After she'd completed her degree, no matter how she'd crunched her numbers, she'd been unable to afford rent *and* a mortgage payment for a building on Main Street. Of course, she'd never imagined that five years later she'd still be living with her parents. She hadn't counted on the effects of an unhealthy economy.

"Ms. Barnes, I understand if you need more time to decide."

Julie shook her head. It didn't matter that Shady Meadows was her favorite place. She needed to be practical. "No, I want it listed this week."

Ms. Morrison smiled broadly. "I'll draw up the contracts this afternoon. Can you meet me in my office tomorrow at noon?"

"I'm not sure," Julie hedged, searching in her oversized canvas bag for her datebook.

One minute she was convinced selling was the right choice. The next minute misgivings eroded her confidence. She longed for her hayloft retreat, her favorite thinking space since childhood, the place where she could always count on uninterrupted time alone with God. Today, she'd have to settle for the drive back from South Wales to Akron. Drawing in a calming breath, she strode toward her ten-year-old Ford Tempo.

The agent hurried to keep up, probably stumbling in her three-inch heels on the gravel driveway. Julie moderated her pace until Ms. Morrison came alongside her.

"I'm not sure I can make it tomorrow. I really have to check my schedule." With her back to the agent, Julie leaned inside the car and shuffled through a crate piled with mail and books. Her disorganized, it's-in-here-somewhere filing system needed a serious upgrade. Giving up her search, Julie straightened and pivoted to face the woman in time to catch her annoyed expression.

"I must have left my datebook at Canine Jewels."

Had she left it on her desk subconsciously? She never went anywhere without her datebook. Disguising her momentary confusion with a practiced smile, she told the agent, "I'll call your secretary in the morning to set up an appointment."

"Certainly, dear." Ms. Morrison laid her cool hand on Julie's bare arm.

Julie flinched, but the older woman appeared not to notice.

"I must advise you not to hesitate, Ms. Barnes. I've already had several inquiries. And, unfortunately, it is a buyer's market now."

Why would Ms. Morrison suggest waiting a few weeks to list the farm if she already had potential buyers lined up? What game was she playing? Julie needed more time to think this through. She thanked the agent, slid into the driver's seat, started her noisy engine, and shifted the car into drive before Ms. Morrison could respond with any more sales tactics.

From the end of the long driveway, Julie stole a quick glance in her rearview mirror. It hadn't rained in over two weeks. Oh, no! She must have hit the gas pedal too hard. A dirt cloud swirled around Maggie Morrison's feet all the way up to the hem of her tailored suit.

Guilt shot with a shiver through Julie. She wasn't usually rude. In fact, she prided herself on considering others' feelings before her own, but the woman's over-eagerness to get her hands on Shady Meadows left a sour taste that made Julie dig into her bag for the tin of strong mints. Her mind whirling with questions, she popped one in her mouth. Should she list the property with a different company? Why would the woman tell Julie to take her time and five minutes later warn her not to hesitate? How could she trust someone who contradicted herself to get a contract?

"What should I do, Lord?"

If only she knew His will. But no clear-cut, immediate answer occurred to her. Too bad she couldn't sit down with Jesus over a pot of coffee and talk it all over with Him. It must have been so much easier for the disciples.

Tamping down her frustration, she switched on the radio. She flipped past classical, country, Christian, and jazz, and settled at last on an oldies station. It had been Aunt Elaine and Uncle Fred's favorite. Nat King Cole was singing "Smile." The song affirmed her belief that crying solved nothing, but in the privacy of her car, Julie allowed herself a few more tears, tears that chilled her face in the cool breeze blowing through her half-open windows. If only she could keep the farm and do right by her brother and her parents.

Wiping tears from her cheeks, she eased up on the accelerator until the speedometer dropped to 45 miles per hour. If she controlled her lead-foot, she'd have a solid forty-minute drive to compose herself. She had work to finish before heading home for dinner. Sunday and Monday were the nights her family ate together. The rest of the week, Julie usually fixed herself something in the small kitchen at Canine Jewels. Sometimes, she met her friends from the ladies Bible study at a local restaurant. If she'd thought ahead and scheduled her meeting with Ms. Morrison for tomorrow night, Julie wouldn't need to hide her ambivalent feelings. But getting the dreaded meeting over with had been her main goal.

As the adage proclaimed, hindsight is 20-20. But it didn't really matter. Whenever she told her parents about her decision, she wanted to be one hundred percent convinced she'd made the right choice. Right now, she wasn't sure.

Lord, if You have a plan I'm missing, please show me what it is because I can't see it.

"Sadie!"

Exhausted from his grueling shift, Buffalo Police Officer Derrick Walker chose to ignore the fact that his sister's seventy-pound German shepherd was already cowering. "Come out from under the table. *Now!*"

The dog refused. With her perfect ears plastered to her head, she looked at Derrick as if he were public enemy number one. He'd seen that expression too many times in the last 72 hours. He was doing this all wrong.

Frustrated as much with his sister as he was with her sorry excuse for a dog, he tried a softer tone. "You have to go out."

The shepherd scooted back against the wall.

Hoping she'd emerge on her own, Derrick shifted onto his heels to give Sadie some space. What had he gotten himself into? He couldn't live three weeks—let alone ten or twelve years—with a dog that shrank in fear at the sight of him. He grabbed Sadie's collar and tugged her out from under the table. "I'm done cleaning up after you."

Annoyed that he'd been forced to pull the trembling dog out the back door, Derrick shook his head in dismay as Sadie darted like a lightning bolt across the fenced yard. They'd gotten off to a horrible start, but he would do whatever it took to make this work for Melanie's sake. Ever since their parents died, Derrick had promised himself he would protect his sister from any more loss.

And God help him, she really loved this dog.

When she'd told him her fiancé was allergic to dander, she'd actually cried. Derrick couldn't take his sister's tears. His response had flown from his mouth. "I'll take her, Sis, and you can visit her anytime you want. She'll still be your dog, but she'll be living with me." He'd hugged Mel and promised, "It'll be all right, you'll see."

With determined steps, Derrick closed the distance between him and the fulfillment of his promise. He sighed as he crouched in the grass to hook the lead to the dog's collar. "Come on, girl," he pleaded. "I'm not such a bad guy. Mel likes me, and you love *her*."

The dog's only response was to back farther away and hide behind the massive oak tree shading the corner of the lot.

Derrick was in trouble. He'd been a cop long enough to know he needed backup. But who?

His cell phone blared some nondescript, tinny tune. He had to change it, he thought for the umpteenth time. Getting to his feet, he retrieved his phone and stifled a groan at his sister's name displayed on the screen. She'd been on her honeymoon for two days, and already she was checking on her precious dog. Derrick considered not answering, but Mel—thinking he was busy on a call or something—would call back. No sense postponing the inevitable.

"Hi, Mel." Trying to keep his voice light, he asked, "How's the weather?" Stupid question. His sister and her new husband were in Hawaii. Of course, the weather was fantastic.

"I'm fine. Bob's fine. What I want to know is, how is Sadie?"

Derrick hesitated. Could he lie to his sister and get away with it? Probably not. Despite the skills he'd acquired on the force, she could still read him. Besides, after the accident, they had made a pact to always tell each other the truth.

"Derrick, are you still there?"

"Yep, I'm here. The fact is your dog's scared to death of me."

"What did you do to her?" Melanie demanded. "You

didn't hit her, did you?"

He hadn't hit Sadie, but he had thought about it. More than once. Especially with her propensity to leave a puddle on the floor every time he looked at her. Or raised his voice. Tonight, he'd come home from work to discover she'd gnawed the corners of two oak cupboard doors, doors he would have to replace if he put his house on the market. He had shouted at Sadie in a tone intended to halt the vilest criminal. Which of course sent the dog scurrying under the table like a frightened rabbit.

"Derrick, what exactly is going on?"

"Look, Mel, I didn't hit your dog. But she doesn't like me."

"Oh." Her tone was both sad and disappointed in him.

Neither of which he could stand. "So, what do I do now?"

Mel said something to her husband Derrick couldn't make out.

"Derrick, do you still have the manila envelope I gave you?"

"Well, yeah, sure, somewhere."

"Great, find the bright orange flyer from Julie's Canine Jewels. Call Julie Barnes. She'll know exactly what to do."

He raked his left hand through his hair. He needed to get it cut ASAP before the chief complained. "Julie's what? I don't think a fancy collar is going to help."

"Julie's Canine Jewels. She's a dog trainer who comes highly recommended by my vet."

Derrick agreed to call Julie, and after a few pleasantries about parasailing and deep-sea fishing, he and Mel ended their conversation with his promise to call her with an update after Sadie had been evaluated.

Twenty minutes later, using a hot dog, he successfully lured the reluctant shepherd to the backdoor. She raced inside ahead of him, fleeing to the safety of her crate and the blanket that still smelled faintly of his sister's perfume. Feeling sorry for Sadie because she hadn't stopped for water, he placed the stainless steel bowl in the front corner of the crate, where he hoped she wouldn't knock it over and make another mess for him to clean up. Two of the three fleece blankets Melanie had provided were already in the washer. Caring for a dog was proving to be almost as much work as caring for a kid, and Derrick had not planned on doing either for a long time, if ever.

The kind of woman who would be best for him didn't exist anymore. The quiet type who didn't ask a man questions about things he'd rather not talk about had disappeared, probably before he was born.

Julie was heading home when her phone rang. Prepared to inform her mother that she didn't have time for an emergency run to the local grocery store,

Julie glanced at the Bluetooth display on the dashboard. She didn't recognize the number, but she figured it was probably business, and she couldn't afford to lose a potential client. She pressed the connect button on the steering wheel. "Good afternoon, Julie's Canine Jewels, how may I help you?"

"Hello, my name is Derrick Walker. I'd like to meet with you as soon as possible. Do you have an opening this evening, say six-thirty?"

Julie recognized the desperation in the man's abrupt manner. People at the end of their resources were usually willing to work with her, which made it so much easier to help their dogs. "I'm sorry, sir, but I have a prior engagement. What exactly are you looking for, a group class, or private lessons?"

"Definitely private lessons."

She detected the veiled embarrassment in his brief reply. And something else she couldn't identify, something that inexplicably drew her to this stranger. "I'm actually closed on Monday nights, but I could meet with you briefly at my school at eight, if that's not too late."

The man sighed with relief. "Great, we'll be there."

She smiled again, glad to focus on business and postpone thinking about the difficult conversation she needed to have with her parents. "Sir?"

"Yes, ma'am?"

She suppressed a groan at the address that made her feel old. "What kind of dog do you have?"

"Sadie's a one-year-old German shepherd."

"I look forward to meeting you both. Do you need the address?"

He recited the address, which she confirmed.

After they disconnected the call, she prayed as she always did for God to give her the wisdom to help this new client and his dog. Failure was not an option for Julie. Ever.

To avoid her mother's keen eyes, Julie decided to hop in the shower before dinner. She wasn't ready to discuss the farm, primarily because Mom would try to talk her out of selling. With a speed rivaling the rate of her years on the high school track team, Julie bolted through the door and raced up the steps. To deflect her mother's suspicions, she hollered from the top of the stairs, "I'll be down to help with dinner as soon as I've had a shower."

"No problem. Everything's under control."

Good. Maybe she could make it through dinner without the subject of her inheritance coming up. Or so she hoped, until Mom said, "Tom, something is bothering Julie. She hasn't been herself for days."

"Liz, Julie is twenty-seven," Dad said. "If she wants to confide in us—"

"But I *know* something is wrong."

"With your busy schedules—"

"I don't need to spend a lot of time with her to see she's upset."

"If you insist, I'll talk with her after dinner. But I want to go on record as stating I'd rather wait until *she* comes to one of us."

As Julie closed the bathroom door and flicked the switch that started the fan's annoying whirr, she thanked God for her new client and his German shepherd. She couldn't possibly stay for one of her father's interrogations. Being the daughter of a police detective had its drawbacks, but Dad never interfered with her work responsibilities. He respected the fact she was an adult with her own life. Mom was the one who had trouble remembering that Julie was perfectly capable of handling life's speed bumps all on her own, thank you very much. She'd survived her breakup with Nick, patched up her life and her heart, and returned home after college to start her own business.

She wasn't opposed to seeking her parents' counsel. But she intended to pray until she knew her own mind on the matter, and hopefully, God's will, before she addressed selling the farm with her parents.

Dad was cross at dinner, but Mom took his irritability in stride. Even when he muttered, "After thirty-five years of marriage, I can't believe you can't cook my steak the way I like it."

Julie was tempted to say something in her mother's defense, but Mom caught Julie's gaze. "Help me put the finishing touches on dessert."

She followed her mother into the kitchen. "Why does Dad have to say such mean things to you?"

Mom gestured for Julie to get the ice cream from the freezer. "Don't be so hard on him, honey. He's had a bad day. A battered wife died on the way to the hospital." Mom cut three slices of strawberry rhubarb pie and passed them to Julie.

She added a scoop of vanilla to each plate. She sympathized with Dad, but why did he sometimes take his frustration out on Mom?

"Your father and his partner were at their house twice before in the last three weeks. Dad couldn't convince her to press charges, and now she's dead."

"I still don't see why he has to take it out on you."

Mom placed the desserts on a serving tray and handed it to Julie. "That's just the way it looks to you."

Mom's sad smile made Julie feel bad for her part in this conversation. Still, she resented what Dad's being on the police force had done to her parents.

Once, in an unguarded moment, Mom had told Julie about how different Dad was when they'd first met, how thoughtful and attentive to her feelings. She had actually described Dad as a sweet guy. According to Mom, Dad couldn't help the way he sometimes acted. It was who he had to be to do his job well. Julie translated that as insensitivity and harshness. The inevitable consequences of being a cop. She loved her dad, but she wished he could leave his cop mode at work.

She would never marry a cop.

She could not live with the tension. Or the fear.

Lord, if it's all right with You, Julie prayed silently as she helped her mother clear the table, *let me marry an ordinary guy, with an ordinary job. And we'll live ordinary lives on Aunt Elaine's farm.*

You're such a romantic, Miss Barnes.

Julie smiled at her acknowledgement. Until she remembered, she was selling the farm. And she would probably never marry. So much for a happily-ever-after life.

Relieved Dad had forgotten his promise to talk to her, Julie left the house determined to set aside her ambivalence about the farm until she'd finished with her new client. As she pulled into the back parking lot, she smiled at her front windows with their beautiful paintings of Labrador, German shepherd, and Yorkie puppies. In bold blue letters, BRINGING OUT THE BEST IN YOUR DOG proclaimed her motto. God had blessed her, enabling her to fulfill her dream of training dogs and protecting their lives in the process. She should be thankful, and joyful, too. So why couldn't she escape the dull ache in her chest, the ache for something more?

At twenty-seven, she was still living with her parents while most of her friends were married and living in their own homes.

As she retrieved the necessary paperwork from the filing cabinet in her office, Julie dismissed her angst as disappointment and frustration over something she couldn't impact at all. There hadn't exactly been a line of eligible Christian men standing at her door. The one man she'd considered had turned out to be a make-believer rather than a believer.

Without her permission, Nick's handsome image flashed in her mind. With his gorgeous blue eyes, ash blond hair and dazzling smile, he had charmed his way into her life and taken control of both her free time and her heart in a few short weeks.

She shook her head. To think she'd once believed he was God's choice for her. After all these years, it still smarted a bit to acknowledge how naïve she had been.

"You were only twenty. You're much wiser now."

But she didn't need to be wise about men. She hadn't given any man a chance since Nick had found a girlfriend who would make him happy.

It didn't matter. Work was Julie's refuge. At Canine Jewels, relationships were built on her terms, based on mutual respect and affection. She truly did have so much to be thankful for.

Besides, plenty of married people she knew were lonely, too.

Julie unlocked the front door, put on a classical CD,

and retrieved her date book from her canvas bag. Striding into her office to check her schedule for available spots, she opened the book and grabbed a pencil.

Yes, after her meeting, she'd found her datebook on her desk. Clearly, her subconscious was trying to tell her she didn't want to sell. She released a snicker. Of course, she didn't want to sell. That was a no-brainer.

Do You care what I want, Lord? I used to think so. Before Aunt Elaine died. But now ...

Letting the gentle classical music soothe her agitated mind, Julie attended to the task before her. On a sticky note featuring puppies of various breeds, she jotted down several options for initial lessons and attached the note to a blank contract. She would scan the signed contract into her computer after the meeting, so she'd have both an electronic and a paper copy.

Derrick Walker arrived promptly at eight. The dog he dragged along behind him weighed about seventy pounds, but the man could have scooped the black and tan shepherd into his arms and carried her inside. In fact, he could probably carry Julie as effortlessly as he could his dog. A blush warmed her cheeks, and she told herself not to stare. Just because the guy had six-pack abs and chiseled features with a fabulous shadow beard was no reason for her to act like an awestruck teenager. She was a professional, a grown woman who'd learned her lesson the hard way.

Besides, she did *not* like the way he was using his

strength to force his dog to go where she clearly did not want to go. Julie had been a trainer for over five years, and she knew his type too well. Harsh and demanding, men like him never seemed to see their dogs as God's fellow creatures. She would have her work cut out for her.

To continue her observations, Julie stationed herself a few feet from the mismatched pair. "Does she always pull on the leash?"

"How should I know?" His blue eyes flashed. "I've only had her for a few days. She's my sister's dog."

"Well, in that case," Julie began, attributing his abrupt temper more to frustration with the dog than with her, "I apologize for bringing you all the way over here, Mr. Walker. But I always work with the owner."

He frowned. "Oh, no, you don't understand, Julie. You are Julie, right?"

She nodded.

"Sadie is my dog now. Ever since my sister married a guy who's allergic to dogs."

Julie resisted the urge to correct him. The man was actually allergic to the dander, not to the dog. "Okay, so back to my question, does she always pull for *you*?"

Derrick's face colored crimson. "Not always. Sometimes she hides under tables or behind furniture. On those days, we don't even get to the leash part. I have a fenced backyard."

He smiled, and Julie concluded he was making a joke to cover his embarrassment. Clearly, he was a man accustomed to controlling his environment and everyone in it. Unfortunately, the frightened eyes of the stunning dog at his side declared that the shepherd had no desire to be controlled in such a heavy-handed manner. The dog's stance told Julie a lot. The only way this dog could make herself look any smaller would be to crouch on the floor, which of course no dog would do in unfamiliar surroundings.

Letting her explore could increase her confidence, and a confident dog was usually a willing student. "Please, release her," Julie instructed.

"What? Let her go? Why?"

Julie suppressed a smile. "Trust me. If we give her a chance to explore and check things out, she'll relax a little. Besides, I need to review some basic information with you before we start."

Derrick assessed her from the top of her head to her scuffed sneakers. What was he doing? Attempting to gauge her physical strength and ability?

This time she laughed outright.

"What's so funny?" he grumbled.

"You are." She swallowed a chuckle. "Thinking physical strength would give me the upper hand with your dog."

He frowned at her, clearly skeptical. Did he think she was nuts? Or incompetent? Maybe both.

Then it hit her. "You're a cop." Julie didn't know how she knew. She just knew. Growing up with her dad, she had learned to recognize the commanding presence.

So much for her thinking Derrick was attractive. That was not a word she was willing to pair with any cop. Especially one as irresistibly handsome as the dark-haired, brooding man before her.

A man you know nothing about.

He shook his head.

How could she be wrong? The shrouded look in his eyes was a cop trademark. The mark of a man who hid more than he revealed. "You're not a cop?"

"I am a cop," he admitted. "And a sergeant in the Army before that. What I'd like to know is how did you figure me out so quickly?" He closed the distance between them until mere inches separated them.

His spicy aftershave wafted to her nose. Her nerves tingled with awareness of him, a growing awareness she had no business entertaining. She drew in a deep breath and let it out. "My dad's a detective on the Buffalo Police force."

Surprised recognition flashed across the hard planes of his far too handsome face. "Detective Tom Barnes is your father?"

"Guilty as charged," Julie said, trying to hide her discomfort with humor, but her heart was racing rebelliously out of control. How could she be attracted to this man, a man who obviously worked in the same precinct as her father? She had decided early on, no cops for her.

Chapter Two

Derrick unhooked Sadie's leash then took the stack of papers Julie held out to him. Always a fast reader, he scanned the documents quickly. It was a standard contract, with one exception. Julie's Canine Jewels guaranteed client satisfaction or a complete refund, provided he complied with her instructions. He stopped himself before he could shake his head. She didn't look like a woman who had to have everything her way. She was definitely not his type, no matter how appealing she might look with Sadie eating kibbles out of her lap. This time he did shake his head. What exactly had she done to bring about such a rapid transformation? Clearly, Detective Barnes' daughter could back up her guarantee.

Derrick signed the contract in the precise hand his mother had taught him so many years ago. Sometimes, he wrote carefully without thinking, out of habit. Other times, he did it for her, and for himself, so he could remember the way her smile had made her face glow whenever he pleased her. But if she were still alive today, he wouldn't be seeing many of her smiles. Derrick gave himself a mental shake. His mother had been dead for fifteen years. The only woman whose smile mattered to him now, and had for years, was Melanie's. And, of course, his grandmother's. Not that he wasn't open to meeting someone special, but casual dating wasn't for him.

Standing at the opposite side of the room from where Julie sat with the dog, Derrick acquainted himself with the curious setup. Three walls were lined with couches and baskets piled high with assorted dog toys. A bookshelf contained, not books, but more toys. The place looked more like a doggie day care than an obedience school. What exactly was her teaching philosophy anyway? Whatever it was, she had made more progress in ten minutes than Derrick had in three days.

He cautiously crossed the room, hoping not to break the spell Julie had cast on Sadie. "What kind of magic are you working?" he asked, slightly irritated *she'd* succeeded in gaining the dog's trust so quickly.

Julie glanced over her shoulder, sending her curly, long blonde ponytail swaying. "Starting a friendship isn't magic, *Officer* Walker. It's an exchange of overtures and a bit of trust."

Ignoring her emphasis on the word officer, Derrick took three more steps toward them. At first, Sadie seemed okay with his approach, but he read her uneasiness in the raised hair across her haunches. He retraced his steps. When the dog visibly relaxed, he made eye contact with the intriguing woman sitting cross-legged on the floor. "Speaking of friendship, please call me Derrick. By the way Sadie responded when I tried to come closer, I'd say we are going to be spending a lot of time together over the next three weeks."

Julie frowned. "Didn't you read the contract? The class runs for a minimum of *eight* weeks."

"I don't have eight weeks."

The lines between her eyebrows morphed to furrows. She stroked Sadie's head, but her gaze never left Derrick's face.

Dialing back his impatience, he tried for a soft, but uncompromising tone. "My sister will be returning from her honeymoon in nineteen days. We have less than three weeks for you to teach me how to gain my dog's trust and cooperation. If you can't promise me Sadie and I will be man and his best friend by then, I'll have to go somewhere else. We have an excellent trainer in our K-9 division, and I'm completely confident—"

"You can't!" Julie jumped to her feet. Sadie stationed herself next to Julie's leg, conveying a united front.

"I beg your pardon." He couldn't believe his ears. They had known each other less than an hour, and she was already ordering him around. How could he possibly work with her? Why on earth had Melanie recommended *this* woman? Maybe because she'd won over his dog at the first meeting. "Are you in the habit of shouting at all your clients?"

"Of course not." She grabbed a yellow lacrosse ball from a nearby basket and rolled it across the room. Sadie ran after the ball, and Julie faced Derrick. "I'm sorry for barking at you like that, but Sadie doesn't have the confidence for police canine training. If you put her in a training program where she can't succeed, you could break her spirit completely."

Derrick held Julie's compelling gaze. Her commitment impressed him. She was formidable, not a quality he had ever admired in a woman before. He strode closer to her until she had to look up to avoid breaking eye contact. For a split second, he actually respected her passion. "Let's forget for a minute how inappropriate and unprofessional you are acting—"

"Unprofessional?" she sputtered. "I'm trying to advise you on what would be best for—"

He held up his hand to stop her words. "Can you help in me in three weeks or not?"

She hesitated. Indecision alternated with determination in her intelligent blue eyes. A moment later, some other emotion that didn't make any sense flashed across her fine-boned face, but she schooled her features and smiled up at him. "I'll do my best. But you'll have to work much harder to see results so fast."

Hard work wouldn't be a problem, as long as he succeeded. Maybe, he'd have to take a couple days off. He had so many sick and personal days racked up he could skip work until Mel got back. But if he did that, he wouldn't find out if Sadie could fit into his real life.

Julie studied him, waiting for his answer.

"We'll both have our work cut out for us. But Melanie will be happy when we succeed."

"Melanie?"

"My sister," he said, extending his hand to shake on their agreement. When Julie placed her hand in his, he couldn't help wishing she were his type. Underneath her tough exterior, something vulnerable and fragile drew him to her. "So, we have a deal, right?"

"We do. But there's one more thing I want you to do." Her tone suggested her final condition might make him change his mind.

"Anything, as long as my dog learns to adore me as much as she adores you."

Sporting an amused grin, she shook her head at him. "That's a lofty goal. But doable if you follow my instructions. For starters, I need you to keep a journal of your interactions with Sadie, and make it as detailed as possible. I'm going to need to know exactly what you're doing wrong."

She smiled again, probably to take the sting from her words. She was clearly a born teacher, always conscious of her responsibility to nurture her student's potential. His mother would have loved her, would have encouraged him to get to know Julie on a personal level. Except Mom wouldn't like the man he'd become. And Julie Barnes was not the kind of woman he would ever consider getting involved with.

"Of course, I want to know what you're doing right, too," she added.

But before he could respond, she launched into detailed instructions for the next twenty-four hours until their first lesson.

He suspected everything Julie wanted him to do with Sadie would tax his patience. Wait, wait, wait. Everything was about him waiting for the dog to respond appropriately. The woman's technique rubbed against the grain of years of training. Authority, submission, and obedience were the keys to an effective team, which is what he and Sadie needed to be if he were going to keep her. Strike that. He had to keep her.

One thing about Julie's approach made perfect sense. He had to teach Sadie to exercise self-control. Self-control was the code Derrick lived by. It had kept him alive in Afghanistan fighting Al Qaeda and alive on the streets of Buffalo's west side.

"Derrick, did you hear what I said?"

Had he zoned out on her? That wasn't good. He was altogether too comfortable around her if she could make him less than one hundred and ten percent aware of his surroundings. Which was one more reason she would be all wrong for him. "I'm sorry. I was thinking all this waiting is going to require a lot of patience. Are you sure it will work?"

Julie smiled. "It has for the last five years."

"Always?"

"Unless the human gives up on the dog," she said without a hint of accusation in her tone.

But the sadness in her soft blue eyes made him want to hold her close until ... until what? Until he could make everything right in both of their worlds? He barely knew this woman. Besides, he had enough on his hands trying to make everything okay for Mel and her timid dog.

"I won't give up on Sadie," he said.

The relief on Julie's face was evident, and Derrick couldn't ignore the happiness coursing through him at her wide smile. "What were you saying when I zoned out on you?"

"We need to check our calendars."

He pulled his cell from his jeans pocket, and together they set up a schedule for their initial sessions.

When it was time for them to leave, Sadie sidled up against Julie's leg and cocked her head. He figured she was probably asking her teacher if she could sleep over. "Sorry, girl." He ran his hand along her flank in his best reassuring manner. "You have to come home with me." To his great relief, Sadie looked up at him in compliance and allowed him to hook her leash to her collar without a fuss.

Maybe, Julie *could* keep her promise to bring out the best in Sadie. Derrick shook Julie's hand again.

Their contact stirred a rush of awareness in him, which he suppressed immediately. Chemistry without compatibility was a recipe for disaster. He thanked her for her time and then tried unsuccessfully to persuade Sadie to walk with him out to the SUV. He gave up, bent down, and scooped her up to carry her. More than likely, Julie would have suggested a better plan, had he been willing to ask.

Six years of being a cop had honed the instincts he had discovered in Afghanistan. He knew without turning around that Julie Barnes was standing in the door watching him, all the way up to the moment he deposited Sadie onto the back seat. The trouble was he couldn't figure out if it was him she was interested in or his dog. Or the way he was handling his dog. Derrick smiled. She had gotten under his skin in a short time, and no woman had done that before.

He started to whistle. Until he remembered she was Detective Barnes' daughter. Which meant she was strictly off limits. Even if he could tolerate her bossiness.

Julie uploaded Derrick's information into her client database. That took all of five minutes. A faint light still shone through her office window. That's what she loved about late June. The longer days meant more opportunities to go running after work. She kept her running shoes and a change of clothes handy, but between her dog school responsibilities and exercising Aunt Elaine's horses, Julie ran only two or three times a week. Tonight was too late for horseback riding, but she could squeeze in a short run before it got dark. A short run would surely eradicate all her errant thoughts of Derrick Walker.

She went into the bathroom and changed into a loose-fitting sleeveless t-shirt and matching white and blue stretch capris. Back in her office, she pulled on cotton socks and her worn running shoes. They needed to be replaced soon, but Julie refused to buy anything on credit. She'd successfully built a solid credit record by not missing a single mortgage payment in five years. She didn't mind being thrifty. Thrifty was safe, though a bit shabby at times. Marla, her best friend from high school, had three pairs of running shoes, one to match each of her favorite colors. But Marla had married into old money. Her husband, Tony, had been handed a readymade, six-figure career by his grandfather as a wedding present. Marla could buy whatever she wanted.

Ugh. Envy was such an ugly emotion. Besides, Julie didn't want Marla's life. Her husband was hardly ever home, and she often complained she felt like a single mom, which was why Marla rarely ran with Julie anymore. Life was full of tradeoffs. From where Julie sat, Marla had traded freedom for financial security.

Julie had given up much of her independence to

establish her business. Why hadn't God made a way for her to have her own home yet? Living with her parents after college hadn't been easy, but recently she'd begun to feel as if her life were locked in a holding pattern. A limited cash flow contributed to the problem, but if she were honest with herself ...

Annoyed, Julie slipped off the pink hair tie and quickly corralled her curls into a loose braid. She snagged a bottled water from the fridge and headed out the front door, locking it behind her. Why was she so aggravated tonight? Putting Shady Meadows on the market and meeting Derrick Walker had both sent her comfortable world dangerously off-kilter. Being attracted to a client, and worse, a cop was totally unacceptable.

Besides, marriage wasn't on her radar.

True, married women often enjoyed the benefits of two incomes, but because Julie had made Canine Jewels her priority, she'd easily discouraged every man she'd met after her breakup with Nick. And for good reason. Without a man, her life was predictable and safe. Emotional security beat financial security, hands down. She needed to feel safe, but what if God's plans for her were bigger than those she had permitted herself?

Startled by that thought, she lifted one foot onto the painted bench outside her door and commenced her stretching routine. Moments later, determined to dismiss all thoughts of the dashing cop, she started off at a slow jog up Main Street.

She'd run the main road through Akron Falls Park then swing back around past the Five Corners. Rose bushes in every conceivable color adorned the well-kept yards of the village residents along her route. She liked the deep red ones best because they smelled the way roses should, like her great-grandfather's prize-winning Lincoln roses.

Julie reveled in the sensations of her body smoothly working in obedience to her commands. She jogged easily past two pre-teens on bicycles. They were clearly in no hurry. For a second, she envied their carefree lives, until she remembered kids had problems, too, problems they often had no means of solving on their own.

Lord, my reaction to Derrick caught me completely off guard. The spark between us can only mean trouble. Please help me to keep my head on straight. I can't make the same mistake twice.

I won't.

I won't get involved with another unbeliever. Especially a cop who works with Dad.

Focusing on the smooth unity of heart, lungs, and muscles, Julie picked up her pace. But blocking out the gorgeous Derrick Walker was not as easy as she had hoped. If he was all wrong for her, why on earth didn't God help her not to think about him?

❀

The following day, Julie decided not to discuss selling the farm with her parents. She planned to sign the realtor's contract sometime tomorrow, but a vague anxiety kept her from making an appointment. The pastor's wife, Katie, would call it a check in her spirit. Could Julie's hesitation be God nudging her in a different direction? Maybe, she'd stop by the parsonage later this afternoon. She hadn't seen Katie in a few weeks, not since the last time Julie volunteered to babysit so the couple could have a night out. Until she'd discussed her reservations with her friend, Julie would follow the pastor's favorite maxim—when in doubt, wait on the Lord. Delaying a decision was better than making the wrong choice, especially about something as important as Shady Meadows.

As she finished entering the notes from the morning classes, her stomach rumbled a raucous complaint. It was twelve-thirty, and Julie needed food, fresh air, and caffeine, not necessarily in that order. She grabbed her canvas bag, flipped the "Closed for Lunch" sign so it was clearly visible in the front door window, locked the door, and headed to her car. She stopped at the deli for a veggie bagel sandwich and a chocolate iced cappuccino. The chocolate would help her shake the gloom dogging her since she'd met with the real estate agent.

Julie drove to the east end of the park and pulled into the lot nearest the path to the falls. She exited the car hoping to hear the soothing rush of water. She sighed at the silence. If it didn't rain soon, the creek bed would dry up to a trickle. How she hated those summers when everyone and everything ached for water. Taking in the fluffy cumulus clouds, she muttered, "God, why do You sometimes withhold Your blessings?"

Feeling awkward, she glanced around to see if anyone had overheard her talking out loud. Nothing and no one were in sight but an empty red pickup and a blue Mustang convertible. Satisfied her reputation as a sensible local businesswoman remained intact, Julie grabbed her lunch and her Bible. As an afterthought, she popped the trunk open and took out a worn blanket. Not wanting to see the dismal state of the falls, she headed down the paved path in the opposite direction toward the lower end of the park. Choosing a shady spot near the edge of Murder Creek, she spread the blanket on the dry grass and sat cross-legged with her Bible by her side and her lunch in her lap. She bowed her head, intending to thank God for the food.

I'm sorry, Lord. I didn't mean to complain. But I don't understand. First, Uncle Fred, and now, Aunt Elaine. I miss them both so much.

Julie ached to tell God she still needed her aunt, still needed the peaceful sanctuary of her aunt's home. But obviously she didn't need Aunt Elaine, or the dear woman would still be here. Julie shook her head, mystified again by God's ways.

She couldn't see any other option to putting the farm up for sale, but maybe the Lord had a different plan.

Encouraged by a spark of hope, she opened her eyes and swigged her iced cappuccino, then bit into her sandwich. Children's laughter diverted her attention from her meal. She scanned the park and spotted a woman pushing a toddler in a baby swing while two small boys climbed the slide. Julie swallowed hard and looked away.

Why couldn't she live at Shady Meadows, by herself? Not having a husband or children didn't mean she couldn't have her own home. Many women enjoyed full, happy lives without ever marrying. Julie had her work, her friends, her family, her church, and most important, God. That would have to be enough.

If only her heart agreed.

If only her traitorous imagination didn't keep conjuring up Derrick.

"He's not the man for you." Saying it out loud should convince her. But it didn't.

Julie refocused her thoughts on something she could control—her decision to sell or not to sell her inheritance. She might be able to manage the taxes on Shady Meadows. If she were careful. Still, it wasn't fair for her to get the farm while her brother got nothing. And she had already agreed to sign the contract. If only God would simply tell her what she should do.

A dog's bark interrupted her troubled thoughts.

"No, Sadie!"

Officer Walker was being dragged across the grass straight toward her. The dog was clearly walking the man, not an uncommon sight, but one that always made Julie smile and reach in her bag for one of her business cards. Sometimes, her offer to help was met with an enthusiastic response. Other times, the rebuff she endured left her shaking her head. Who could understand why people reacted so defensively?

At least this time the party in question was already her client. But she wasn't prepared to see *this* client today. Not when she couldn't get him out of her head.

Accepting the inevitable and hoping she could maintain her professional distance, she dropped her sandwich back into the takeout bag and rose to her feet. In seconds, Sadie and her red-faced owner skidded to an abrupt halt a few feet from Julie and her blanket.

"How nice to see you." She covered her mouth, stifling a chuckle. "Did you bring your lunch?"

He was carrying a brown paper bag, a bit crushed, probably a byproduct of his struggle to control the shepherd. "I did. It seemed like a good idea, bringing Sadie with me, but ...."

Noting his discomfort, Julie sought to put him at ease. "Most new dog owners don't realize walking a dog is not as easy as some people make it look."

"You don't have to tell me. That's another reason I need your help." He smiled and his blue eyes sparkled in the sunlight.

Where was the shrouded look of yesterday? This man could change her thinking about cops, and men in general, if she let her guard down.

Which won't matter at all if he's not a Christian.

Had that been her own thought or God's voice? Either way, she planned to keep her relationship with the handsome cop strictly business. "Have you started your journal?"

His smile turned sheepish. "Not yet. Do you mind if Sadie and I join you for lunch?"

Before Julie could reply, the shepherd lunged for the bag containing the veggie bagel and chips. Derrick yanked the dog to his side with a firm, "Sadie, no."

Pleased that he hadn't used an overly harsh tone. Julie smiled at Derrick. "We better relocate to a picnic table."

"I agree."

"But first we need to reward Sadie for listening to you and returning to your side." Julie retrieved a dog biscuit from her pocket and handed it to Sadie who gingerly took it from Julie's open palm. "Good girl." When the dog finished the biscuit, Julie scratched Sadie's head between her ears. "Good girl."

Derrick gave Julie a dubious look.

"Praise her as much as possible, Officer Walker. She really does want to please you, no matter how much you may think she dislikes you."

"Dislikes me?" Derrick gathered up her lunch and handed it to her. "I never said that."

She picked up the Bible and started to toss the blanket over her arm, but he took it from her, folded it neatly, and passed it back to her.

It was such a simple gesture, but she hadn't had a man, other than her brother or her dad, do anything for her since she'd dated Nick., and he had wanted more in return than she was willing to give. She shuddered to think how close she'd come to crossing that line. Vowing never to put herself in that position again, she'd kept her promise by swearing off men.

Which had been fairly easy until last night.

With his brows drawn together in a disapproving frown, Derrick studied her. "You were insinuating I said my dog dislikes me."

"Not exactly. I know you didn't say that. But it's what you think," Julie explained. "And what's worse Sadie thinks *you* don't like her."

The shrouded look was back in his eyes. "I like her as much as I like any dog."

Hiding her distress at Derrick's admission, Julie ran her hand along the shepherd's back, pleased Sadie didn't mind being touched. The dog had obviously been well loved by Derrick's sister. Perhaps, part of the problem he was having with Sadie stemmed from her feeling abandoned by her former owner.

Julie met Derrick's gaze. "She needs you to love her."

He averted his face, but not before she'd caught his discomfort.

"Is that part of your standard instructions?"

She stepped into his line of vision so he had to make eye contact with her. "No, it's the foundation. If you want her to obey you, she needs to trust you, and trust begins with love."

His closed-off expression told her a lot. He was a man with a past, a past that made it difficult for him to commit to loving even a dog. On the other hand, he loved his sister enough to give her dog a home. Derrick wasn't a man Julie could read easily. Which was another cop trademark. An asset on the job, but, in her opinion, a distinct liability in one's personal life. With a woman or a dog. Part of a good cop's arsenal was the ability to create exactly the right demeanor for every situation.

Which reminded her entirely too much of Nick.

Reining in her thoughts, she refocused her attention on the man in front of her. "Let's sit a while, and enjoy this beautiful day while we eat. You can tell me what you expect from Sadie, what you need her to do so you can live together peacefully."

Derrick tied Sadie's leash around a table leg, and for the next half hour, they discussed his expectations, finally deciding to focus first on getting the dog to go outside willingly. He would enter the house, calmly and quietly greet Sadie, unlock her crate, then wait for her to approach him. When she came to his side, he would reward her with lavish praise and a piece of dog food. They agreed it would be best to postpone their first lesson until Friday. That would give him three days to work on making Sadie feel more comfortable with him before they began teaching her the self-control she needed to build her confidence.

"I enjoyed having lunch with you, Julie," Derrick said as he gathered up their garbage. "I hope we didn't interrupt anything."

"Not a bit." Julie had nearly forgotten her blue mood, the one he had effectively banished with his deep voice and his warm laughter. He was pretty easy on the eyes, too. And she liked a man who could laugh at himself, something she didn't think most cops ever did. "I enjoyed having lunch with you, too, Officer Walker."

"I thought we settled this yesterday." He dropped the garbage in the trashcan then met her eyes. "Call me Derrick. Unless I'm working, only my cleaning lady calls me Officer Walker."

"Is that an order?" She was half teasing, but teasing was outside the parameters of what she considered professional behavior.

Before she could retract her statement, he stepped toward her and took her hand in his. "No, it's a request, an overture of friendship."

Her face heated with the spark arcing between them. She should withdraw her hand, but she was mesmerized by those entrancing blue eyes. "Derrick, I think we'd better remember—"

"Remember what, Julie?"

She swallowed hard. Pulled her hand free. "That you're a cop, and I'm a cop's daughter. And we both know how cops feel about their daughters dating cops."

Which was an easier reason to accept than

acknowledging her fear. Her judgment had failed her once before, and if she were honest, her heart still bore the scars.

❃

As he untied Sadie from the table, Derrick tried to dismiss what Julie had said. But she was right. Anything personal between them would be like walking down a dark alley with no backup. Someone could get hurt. Badly.

Except ...

"There's no law that says we can't be friends," Derrick argued, though he wanted more than friendship from her.

Which doesn't make sense because she's not my type at all. She asks too many questions, and she digs too deep.

"All right, we can be friends." Julie bent down to pat the dog. "You and Sadie and I."

Lumped in with the dog. It was a start.

For the second time in two days, he wanted to hug her, but he resisted the impulse and shook her hand again. "I'll see you Friday at four-thirty."

"Goodbye, Derrick."

Her radiant smile cheered his weary heart. He hadn't realized it, but he was worn out, probably from working so many long hours for too many years. Maybe it was time to reconsider his choice of a non-existent social life.

Enjoying the warmth sparking between them, he reluctantly released her hand. "Have a nice day, Julie."

And don't forget to think about me. Because I'll be thinking about you.

"You, too," she said.

Walking away from Julie, with Sadie pulling him along at the same fast pace as before, was hard. He wasn't used to being embarrassed. Being tough and controlling his emotions were essential. Losing control could mean his life or someone else's.

But when he was around the pretty dog trainer, he wanted to explore rather than control his feelings. The fact was he could easily fall for her.

And ruin her life. She deserved better than to be stuck with a man with enough baggage to fill a Bradley. She deserved an ordinary guy who worked a regular job and could come home to her every night and tell her all about his day. Not a guy with violent, angry memories he preferred to forget.

If he were still a praying man, Derrick would have asked God to help him not fall in love with her. Better yet, he'd have asked God to make sure she didn't fall in love with him.

Chapter Three

That night, alone in her bedroom, when she finally had more than a spare minute to think about anything other than work, Julie forced herself to face the truth. The chemistry between her and Derrick was undeniable. She could kick herself. Or chow down on a slice of chocolate cheesecake. How could she be attracted to a cop? She flopped onto her bed, and burying her face in her pillow, released a groan. Seconds later, she jumped up and paced the room until she caught sight of herself in the mirror.

Ugh! "Get your act together, girl."

Overwhelmingly frustrated, she knelt beside her bed to pray. "Lord, why did he have to be a cop? Couldn't you have sent someone else? Like a mechanic or a doctor or a librarian? Anybody but a cop. And he works in the same precinct with Dad. What were you thinking, God?"

God did not answer. Possibly because her prayer sounded more like a rant.

She resumed pacing. She hadn't really expected an answer. After Aunt Elaine had died of brain cancer in January, Julie had stopped listening for answers, fearful of what further heartache might be in store for her. What if God saw her as a difficult daughter, one who could only learn her spiritual lessons from hard things? At this moment, she couldn't think of anything harder than being over-the-top attracted to a guy who was all wrong for her.

She undid her braid and ran her fingers through the crimped locks, then pulled on a pair of pink-striped pajama pants and a faded mint green t-shirt. "Sure, I know 'all things work together for good,' but a cop, Lord? I could never be happy with a cop. After years of listening to Mom pacing the floors, praying for Dad, sobbing with relief when he finally made it home.... Not to mention putting up with his bad moods. I promised myself I'd never marry a cop. So, I shouldn't get involved with him."

Derrick hadn't asked her out. Yet. But he wanted more than friendship. She'd seen it in his eyes and felt it in his touch. Working with him was going to be a real challenge.

She had friends who dated casually, but Julie had decided, back in high school, never to date anyone she didn't think would be a good partner. And a cop was definitely not the father she wanted for her kids. She'd believed a veterinarian would be a perfect husband and a wonderful dad, but she couldn't have been more wrong about Nick.

Could she be wrong about Derrick? No, he was a cop, and being married to a cop came with challenges she couldn't handle. It was hard enough being a cop's daughter. She shook her head at her reflection in the mirror. "You will never date a cop. No matter how attracted you are to Derrick Walker. Stick with the plan. No cops. Ever."

Startled by a knock at her door, she collided with the corner of her dresser and banged her upper thigh. She bit her lip to hold back the cry of pain.

"Julie, may I come in? I forgot to ask you something at dinner last night."

Great! Had her mother overheard anything? When would Julie ever learn to stop talking to herself? Sure, she was a grown woman, and who she was willing to date was her own business. But somehow her aversion to dating a cop felt like betrayal.

Lord, I could use a little help, more than a little, if Mom heard what I said about never dating a cop.

Julie pasted a smile on her face, opened the door to invite her mother inside, then retreated to her four-poster bed. Hoping to avoid an unpleasant conversation, she sat cross-legged, absently stroking the smooth, cotton wedding ring quilt, and released a perfectly timed yawn.

"I forgot to mention to you yesterday," Mom said, remaining in the doorway, "Katie wanted me to ask you if you would make your chocolate peanut butter cupcakes for the youth group bake sale this Saturday."

"The bake sale is this week? I thought it was next week. I was actually planning to visit Katie this afternoon, but my day got away from me." Lunch with Derrick and Sadie had put Julie behind at work, but time wasn't the real problem. She had completely forgotten her plan to talk with Katie about selling Shady Meadows. Her unplanned attraction to Derrick was the current problem with a capital P.

Mom's astute gaze suggested that probing questions were coming. Was she a mind reader? Julie casually touched her cheek to check for the heat of a blush. She held her breath. Talking about Derrick Walker with her mom wouldn't accomplish anything.

"What should I tell Katie? Do you have time to bake cupcakes this weekend?"

Relieved her mom must not have overheard anything Julie had said about not dating a cop, she pursed her lips and pretended to consider Mom's request. Baking would be a relaxing distraction. Besides, the pastor's wife rarely asked for any special favors. "Sure. I'd be glad to bake cupcakes. I'll make a double batch. Last time, they sold out so fast Pastor Steve didn't get one."

Mom laughed. "I remember. I'd never seen him pout

before. Not in the ten years he's been our pastor."

"You're right." The whole church knew about Pastor Steve's weakness for sweets. He was a regular judge of the annual pie baking contest held at the church's summer picnic, but last year, he'd declared Julie's chocolate peanut butter cupcakes the best dessert he'd ever eaten. Not the competitive type, his wife took this declaration in stride. With three toddlers, she rarely had time to bake, except the occasional boxed brownies for guests.

"I'll call Katie in the morning and tell her I'll not only bake my cupcakes, but I'll put a dozen aside for their family."

"That's sweet of you. You might want to set some aside for your dad. They're his favorite, too, remember?"

"Of course." Julie grinned. "That won't be a problem. I can get up early on Saturday morning, bake the cupcakes, drop them off at church, and still be at the farm to exercise the horses by ten."

"I've been meaning to ask you ..." Mom perched on the end of the bed. "What do you plan to do about Shady Meadows?"

"I haven't decided." Julie leaned against the headboard and hugged her knees to her chest. She couldn't avoid having this conversation with one or both of her parents. "I'm still praying about it. But, honestly, I really don't know what to do."

Mom scooched close enough to brush her fingers over Julie's knee. "Sometimes, God speaks to us through other people, honey."

Julie knew where this was going. "I know that, Mom. And I know you mean well, but—"

"Your dad and I want you to keep the farm." Mom's firm tone suggested they had discussed at length what should be done with her sister's beautiful property.

But it wasn't their decision to make. "What we want isn't always possible."

"With God, everything is possible, Julie."

"I believe that. But not if what we want is outside His will." Julie had wanted Aunt Elaine to beat brain cancer, but she still died. "Can we talk about this later, Mom? I'm exhausted."

Hurt and disappointment clouded her mother's eyes. "Remember, honey, you can still talk to me about anything. Anytime."

Julie wanted to remind her mother that she was twenty-seven, not seventeen, but she nodded, and brushed a kiss across her mother's cheek. "Goodnight, Mom."

"Goodnight."

Relieved, Julie closed her bedroom door.

Julie's alarm sounded at 6:00 a.m., but she didn't leap out of bed the way she normally did.

On Wednesday mornings, she kept her calendar free for personal appointments, errands, and extra time with the horses. Today, thankfully, she had nothing scheduled. She sat up in bed and picked up her Bible from the nightstand with one thought on her mind. She had to make the right choice about the farm. She couldn't do that if she couldn't hear from God. She opened her Bible to John chapter ten. "Lord, guide me. I can't trust my own judgment." She gravitated to her favorite verse, John 10:27. Julie had highlighted it in yellow way back when she was trying to decide which college to attend. Too bad she hadn't paid more attention to this verse when she'd first met Nick. She could have saved herself a lot of heartache.

"My sheep hear my voice, and I know them, and they follow me." Reading the words aloud usually helped to ground her in the truth, but today, thoughts of Derrick and Shady Meadows tumbled in her head like a Fisher Price popcorn popper.

She tried to meditate on the verse, to acknowledge the words as a truth she'd proven for herself, but her mind plagued her with questions. Was this a promise? Or a statement of fact? Were there conditions? Conditions she might not be meeting? What did God expect from her?

She didn't have time to be plagued with indecision. She'd already postponed calling the agent. Ms. Morrison had left two messages on Julie's voicemail yesterday afternoon. Julie didn't normally ignore voicemail messages, but she couldn't allow the real estate agent to influence her decision. Julie needed to do what was right for her. Unfortunately, in this case, what was right for her wouldn't be fair to her parents or to her brother. No matter what Mom thought. Unless Julie could make up the difference to her brother. Somehow.

Julie ignored the anxiety churning in her stomach. She showered then dressed in worn, baggy jeans, her favorite purple t-shirt, and her barn sneakers. She put her riding boots in her canvas bag and headed downstairs for coffee. She'd make herself an egg sandwich and eat it in the car on the way out to the farm.

Although it was barely seven-thirty, both her parents had already left for the day. She loved having the kitchen to herself on Wednesday mornings. The rest of the week they tripped over each other trying to get out the door. If it weren't for the fact that the three of them were rarely home together, Julie would have found a way to move out by now. Keeping Shady Meadows would give her parents back their privacy. Plus, caring for the horses and maintaining the property on site would be so much easier than it had been these last five months, even with a forty-five-minute commute from South Wales to Akron.

Although she was eager to get out to the farm, Julie decided to stop by the parsonage first. She pulled her cell from her pocket and scrolled through her contacts until she found Katie's number.

"Good morning, Katie. This is Julie Barnes."

Katie chuckled. "I know your voice. Actually, I was

expecting your call."

Julie remembered the bake sale. "Oh, yeah. Cupcakes. I can definitely bake my chocolate peanut butter cupcakes. Put me down for a double batch."

"That's great. Steve can't stop talking about how delicious they are."

Julie took a deep breath. "That's not really why I called. If you're not busy, I'd like to stop by for coffee and a chat this morning."

Katie quickly agreed, and Julie ended the call. The rest of what she had to say was best discussed in person.

Twenty minutes later the two of them were sitting in the parsonage's backyard in the shade of a picnic umbrella while Katie's three boys played in the sandbox with their trucks. Peace reigned for the moment, but Julie knew from babysitting the boys that disputes occurred regularly. "Katie, I'm sure you have a lot on your schedule today, and I need to get out to the farm."

Katie glanced up from stirring cream and sugar into her coffee. Her welcoming smile put Julie at ease. "Let's focus on what you came to talk about."

Julie liked Katie's directness. But the right words wouldn't come.

Katie slid a tray of cut-up fruit toward Julie. "I was praying for you this morning. Your mom called last night to tell me you were planning to sell your aunt's place."

Julie ignored her increasing frustration with her

mother.

"Why do you want to sell?" Katie tucked a strand of long brown hair behind her ear. "You've always told me Shady Meadows was your favorite place in the world."

Julie picked up a chunk of mango and chewed it slowly as she collected her thoughts. "I need to divide the profits with my brother and my parents." That was it in a nutshell. There wasn't anything more to say on the subject.

Katie's smile disappeared. "You're not happy with your decision."

Julie averted her face and pretended to watch the boys negotiating over a dump truck filled with superhero figures. "That's beside the point."

"I disagree."

Returning her attention to her friend, Julie met Katie's determined gaze with stubborn resolve. "You don't think I should share the profits? It's the only fair thing to do."

Katie leaned across the glass top table. "I disagree with your premise that your happiness is beside the point."

Julie sipped her coffee then crossed her arms under her chest. Feeling like a petulant teen, she unfolded her arms and rested her hands in her lap. "I won't be happy unless I do the right thing. And God won't be happy with me."

"And you think selling is the right thing to do? Your reasons may be sound, but your distressed expression tells me your heart doesn't agree."

Julie was about to deny this, but the two older boys were tumbling in the grass, and the youngest was trying to pull them apart. Shouts of "Mom" filled the air.

Katie jumped into action. She placed the older boys in time-out under two shady maple trees at opposite corners of the fenced lot. That left the youngest with no one to play with for the next five minutes. Katie brought him to the picnic table, strapped him in a booster seat, and handed him a napkin with three mango chunks and two apple slices. "Jeremy, please eat quietly while Mommy and Miss Julie are talking."

The two older boys chorused, "We want fruit, too."

"When you are finished with your time-outs."

To Julie's amazement the boys accepted this without further comment. Katie was a fantastic mom. She didn't yell or threaten, but her children respected her authority. Would Julie ever experience the joy of motherhood? Unbidden, Derrick's face popped into her head. But a cop was not the father she wanted for her kids.

"God wants to give you the desire of your heart, Julie," Katie said firmly.

"But what if what I want is not His will?"

"Discovering God's will isn't always easy, especially about something the Bible doesn't address directly. But we know we're in His will when we have peace about our decision." Katie's gaze locked with Julie's. "And I can see you don't have peace about selling Shady

Meadows."

By the time Julie arrived at the farm, it was nearly ten o'clock. Their nearest neighbor, Jared Kramer, had already fed the horses. A quick glance to the east told Julie he had decided to cut the hay today. Jared had been cutting their hay in exchange for half the yield ever since Uncle Fred's death two years earlier. When Aunt Elaine died, Dad had asked Jared to care for the horses until the estate was settled. Now that the property was officially hers, Julie intended to pay Jared for all the work he'd done. She waved in his direction, but he didn't wave back. Maybe he hadn't seen her.

Inside the barn, she greeted the horses, gave them each half an apple, then saddled up her favorite Paint, a ten-year-old mare named Autumn. Her brother, Jack, had come up with the name, though he never enjoyed the horses as much as she did. How would Jack feel if she decided to live here rather than selling? He'd be home in a week for the Fourth of July celebration. She already knew what he'd say. Her little brother had always put her happiness first, even when they were kids. Despite Jack's allergy to dog dander, he'd insisted she keep her sweet Lab puppy. But the pup had died soon after.

Dismissing thoughts of Jack and Toby, Julie stroked the horse's chestnut and white neck then swung her right leg over the saddle to mount Autumn. Riding as one with her horse toward the winding trails in the apple grove, Julie sighed with pleasure. The warm breeze caressed her cheeks as a chorus of birds sang in the nearby trees.

On the back of a horse, with the sun on her face, and a song in her heart. That's how Julie had spent every summer since her tenth birthday. Could she really give this up? Would God require such a sacrifice?

"Lord, show me what to do, please. Katie's right. I haven't had a moment's peace since I took the real estate agent out to the farm."

Autumn whinnied.

"Thanks for your sympathy, girl." She patted the horse's neck. "Time for me to let you have free rein." With a gentle tap of her boots on the horse's flanks, they were racing through the mowed rows between the trees. She leaned slightly forward in the saddle and gave herself over to the rhythm of Autumn's powerful strides.

Ten minutes later, Julie slowed Autumn to a walk. "Let's head back to the barn, girl," she instructed as she gave a slight tug on one rein to turn the Paint around. "Your friends are waiting for their turn."

She glanced at her watch. Was there time to work one more horse before her first lesson of the day at two o'clock?

Two and a half hours left to brush down Autumn, ride and brush down Steadfast, shower, and drive into town. Drive—forty-five minutes. Shower and change—

fifteen minutes. Brushing down the horses—twenty minutes. Unsaddling Autumn, saddling and unsaddling Steadfast—ten minutes. That left an hour. She'd ride Steadfast for forty minutes. Leaving twenty minutes grace time for the unexpected. Julie preferred to always be prepared for the unexpected.

You can't plan for everything.

No, she couldn't. But she could sure try.

By six o'clock on Thursday evening, Julie was willing to admit the truth. Planning for the unexpected worked only if one had already anticipated all the possible contingencies. Never in a million years would she have imagined a sallow-faced ten-year-old would vomit all over his five-month-old Golden Retriever, who in less than a minute would roll and smear the orange mess all over the training room carpet. Neither could Julie have predicted that this unfortunate gastro accident would evolve into an epidemic of crying and gagging children.

She made a mental note for the future—limit puppy classes with children to five clients, period. No exceptions. Ever.

The child's mother had offered to pay to have the indoor/outdoor carpet shampooed, but Julie had declined, though she had second thoughts later when she realized she'd have to reschedule her three remaining lessons. Fortunately, she had a standing arrangement with Carpet Miracle Cleaners, who squeezed her in at the end of their workday. It was nine-thirty by the time they pulled out of the parking lot. Too late for running or horseback riding. At least the rug would be dry for her first appointment at nine the next morning.

Tempted to indulge in a sweet treat, Julie ignored her craving for a hot fudge sundae, headed directly home, and then ran a hot bath scented with her favorite lavender bath oil. She grabbed the latest Christian romance she'd started reading the previous night, put a Debussy CD in the player, stripped off her clothes, and sank deep into the soothing water for a long soak. Within minutes, she'd cleared her head of the day's frustrations and problems and focused on the romance unfolding on the page.

But Derrick Walker crossed her mind several times as she read the World War II love story between a field nurse and a wounded sergeant. Frustrated again, she dropped the paperback onto the thick bathroom rug then proceeded to shampoo her hair with unnecessary rigor. When would she enjoy her own romance? Could the irresistibly handsome cop possibly be the man for her? Probably not. She did like him, and she couldn't deny their mutual attraction. Maybe, some cops could separate their work from their home life. Maybe Derrick was nothing like her dad.

Nagging anxiety extinguished the tiny spark of

hope. If she could come to terms with Derrick's occupation, she still had a bigger problem. She'd misjudged Nick, thinking his church attendance implied a relationship with Christ. She wouldn't make the same mistake with Derrick.

She laughed. She was getting way ahead of herself. Derrick had suggested friendship. Nothing more.

Too bad the same couldn't have been said for Nick.

Looking back, Julie figured she'd never had a prayer of chance of resisting Nick. At least that's the way she reasoned it out on the days she wanted to let herself off the hook. Other days, she berated herself. Any rational woman in her right mind would have recognized what was painfully obvious in retrospect. Nicholas Allen Kensington was a consummate actor. And she, Julie Elaine Barnes, had provided his most receptive and adoring audience ever.

If she were honest, prayer, or rather her lack of prayer had everything to do with why she had succumbed so easily to Nick's charms.

It had been raining for two weeks straight the day Nick asked her to go for coffee.

She'd noticed him from the first morning of her favorite class. They were both taking Animal Behavior, which meant they shared a love for animals. Julie viewed this as a precipitous beginning, possibly a sign, though her father always said believers who searched for signs could be easily tripped up by the devil. She didn't like to think of the devil as that formidable an enemy. At least she hadn't back then, when she was a dewy-eyed twenty-year-old waiting for the love of her life to find her and carry her off to happily-ever-after. From the time she was a little girl, she'd planned to open her own obedience school for dogs. So, it made perfect sense to her that God would plan on her marrying someone who loved dogs as much as she did.

Seventeen students attended Dr. Klein's first lecture on Animal Behavior, but by the second week, only thirteen people were still coming to class, six girls and seven guys. Three girls sat in the row behind Nick. Why he ignored them eluded her. Maybe, he didn't like gigglers. Or freshmen. Or cheerleader types. Or ... what did it matter what type he liked? He obviously didn't like serious girls who knew exactly what they wanted and were willing to work as hard as necessary to achieve their goals. He probably didn't like the competition. Nick was planning to be a veterinarian, and pre-vet students had their fill of competition, didn't they?

At the end of class, Julie stuffed her textbook and her loose-leaf binder into her backpack and turned around to face the biggest surprise of her life.

Nick Kensington was gazing at her with his incredible blue eyes and brilliant smile. "Would you like to go to the Student Union for coffee?"

At first, she couldn't find her voice. "Sure," she agreed, though she'd never drunk coffee in her life. It was the first of many concessions she would make for

Nick.

He reached for her backpack and slung it effortlessly over one shoulder. Before she'd realized what was happening, he had maneuvered her into the crook of his other arm and was guiding her across campus, holding a large, navy umbrella over the two of them. She'd seen couples walking to and from class, standing so close and cozy under giant umbrellas that shut out the frequent rain, and other students, too. Impossibly romantic and devoted to one another, she envied those couples their happiness. And now she was walking with Nick Kensington's arm around her shoulder like those other picture-perfect couples.

The trouble was nothing was perfect about their relationship.

Julie rinsed her hair, finished her bath, and toweled off before slipping into her pajamas. She brushed her teeth and headed to bed. She adjusted the fan up two levels, draped her quilt over the oak rack, and climbed into bed to read another chapter or two of the sweet romance.

"Lord, help. This time let me follow Your lead. If Derrick doesn't know You, help me keep our relationship professional, with no complications caused by my longing for romance. Even though I sometimes complain about being alone at my age, I really am willing to wait for You to bring the perfect man into my life."

The perfect man for her would be devoted to Christ.

Easy on the eyes would be a sweet bonus.

Despite his good looks, Derrick Walker couldn't possibly be that man. And wanting it wouldn't make it so.

For now, she'd have to settle for reading someone else's love story.

Chapter Four

On Friday afternoon, Derrick arrived punctually for his first lesson. He shot Julie a relaxed smile as Sadie struggled against his unrelenting grip. "Hi, Julie."

She tried to slow her racing heart. It wouldn't do at all for him to realize the effect he had on her. She straightened her back, as if somehow perfect posture would make her appear more professional.

Focus on the dog, Julie. Forget the guy. As if.

"Hi, Derrick. Hi, Sadie. You're right on time."

How exactly did he organize his day to arrive on the minute? She was always either a few minutes early or late. Running her own business required her to be a clock watcher, though that wasn't her nature. But after Nick, she'd trained herself to abide by her long list of obligations and rules. A trainer should be on time for every appointment. If possible, appointments should begin and end on time. A professional should *not* be attracted to a client. A cop's daughter should not date a cop. She should not be attracted to a cop.

Even if he did look amazing in jeans and a blue shirt that matched his eyes. Revise that. Especially if he looked amazing in jeans and a t-shirt that matched his incredible blue eyes.

What was with her and blue-eyed men?

She reined in her wandering thoughts and bent to greet the German shepherd by holding her palm out and fingers folded in for the dog to sniff. Ordinarily, she wouldn't approach a dog head-on at the beginning of the first training session, but she'd had enough contact with this intelligent animal to know Sadie remembered her and liked her. After all, they'd shared a picnic. "Hi, Sadie girl."

The dog responded by sniffing and licking Julie's fingers. Julie caressed the dog from her shoulders to her tail. Stroking the shepherd's luxurious coat grounded Julie in the task at hand.

Certain she had her unwelcome attraction to Derrick under control—at least for the moment, Julie allowed herself to gaze directly into his eyes. "I'm pleased to see how much more relaxed Sadie is with you."

He grinned. "You and me both."

He really did have a terrific smile. She was a sucker for a great smile. Even on a cop. On this one particular cop. So much for getting her attraction under control. The heat of a blush threatened to stain her cheeks.

"Your instructions made all the difference." Derrick patted the shepherd's head, breaking eye contact with Julie.

She reminded herself that her dad would have a fit if he found out she were considering dating a cop.

"I don't know why *I* didn't think of letting Sadie take the lead in our relationship. She always was a good dog for Mel."

Probably because you're a take-charge kind of guy. Like every other cop I know.

"I've had no trouble getting her to go outside. She doesn't hide from me or cower anymore either." Derrick smiled at Sadie. "And most importantly, accidents are a thing of the past."

"That's great news." Julie didn't look up from the preliminary progress notes she was adding to Sadie's file.

Derrick eyed her clipboard. "Do we get an 'A'?"

"You get a 'D.'"

He scowled. "Why exactly do we get a 'D'?"

"Because Sadie is developing the skills she needs to be a well-socialized, confident, and obedient dog."

"Right. 'D' for developing."

Julie nodded, hoping to hide her embarrassment. She'd been flirting. He might not have recognized it, but she couldn't deny it. Something about him made her want to trash her rules. But that wouldn't be wise.

"Now that you and Sadie are getting along, we can begin obedience training. Tonight, we'll start on the four essential commands: sit, look, stay, and come. Release her, so we can get started."

"Sounds good." Derrick reached down and unhooked the leash from Sadie's collar. Within seconds, she took off, racing around the perimeter of the training room. Until she skidded to an abrupt halt in the exact spot where last night's gastric accident had soiled the carpet.

Disgusted, Julie shook her head. The rug still smelled. She'd have to call Carpet Miracle Cleaners and have them come back out and treat the area again.

Derrick's face colored crimson. "I'm sorry. I know she's supposed to stay beside me when I unhook her leash."

"That's why we're going to start with a sit-stay command."

He frowned at Sadie, who tilted her head at her owner. "I don't think she's ready for anything that complex."

His dismay tugged at Julie's heart. Being at a loss was clearly out of character for him. And he'd come in today so confident. She squeezed his bare arm, and electricity sparked between them. Suppressing a gasp building in her throat, Julie quickly withdrew her hand and turned away to hide the blush warming her face.

"We do this one command at a time, starting with sit," she said, unwilling to meet Derrick's eyes. To regain her composure, she focused on Sadie, extending her hand palm up with her fingers closed over a piece of dog kibble. Next, she held her hand over the dog's nose high enough so Sadie would have to sit to make contact with her closed hand. "Sadie, sit," Julie commanded.

And Sadie sat.

Derrick resisted the urge to gape at Julie. She made training the shy German shepherd look easy. True, she'd been doing this for over five years, and he'd started working with Sadie only four days ago. *Patience, man. It's her job to teach you what she knows.*

"I'm impressed. Good girl, Sadie."

His dog tilted her head again and focused her liquid brown eyes on him with something akin to warmth. Their relationship had already improved dramatically. With Julie's help, he would be able to keep his promise to his sister.

"Your turn, Derrick." Julie slipped kibbles into his hand.

The brief contact of her warm fingers against his palm sent a surge of electricity through him. He ignored his reaction. Whatever was going on between them, she'd made it clear they couldn't be more than friends. She claimed it was because he was a cop, and she was a cop's daughter, but he sensed more to her desire to keep him at a distance than she was willing to name. At least at this point. Which was okay because he was guaranteed three more weeks to spend with her.

He walked over to Sadie, positioned himself in front of her, and held a piece of kibble in his closed hand the way he'd seen Julie do. "Sadie, sit."

Sadie did not sit. Flabbergasted, Derrick raised his hands in disgust, and the food dropped to the floor. Sadie gobbled up the kibble and faced him with triumph gleaming in her brown eyes. Ignoring Julie's muffled chuckle, he repeated the procedure, this time holding his hand higher over the dog's head. Sadie sat, and he rewarded her with a piece of food. "Much better, girl."

Julie wrote more notes on the lined paper on her clipboard. "You're going to want to use the same words to mean the same thing in similar situations," she advised in what he'd come to recognize as her firm, no-nonsense tone. "Good dog or good girl would be better."

He nodded and stroked the dog between her ears. "Good girl, Sadie."

After ten minutes of practicing sit and sit-stay, they advanced to teaching the shepherd to come on command. Under Julie's tutelage, Sadie's response rate increased from an initial 25 percent to 100 percent in less than 20 minutes. Derrick and Sadie were finally in sync, buoyed forward by the momentum of their shared success.

He couldn't keep from grinning. "What's next?"

Her smile lit up her sun-kissed features. "Look."

She was amazingly beautiful. He could spend all day looking at her. "Look at what?"

She laughed. "At you, of course. You need to be able to gain your dog's attention instantly on command. *Look* works well. But some owners prefer *watch me*."

"Which do you prefer?" He was more than willing to follow her lead if it meant he'd see more of her beautiful smile.

She studied him with a quizzical expression, as if she could read his thoughts. But he couldn't be that transparent, could he?

"When it comes to commands, one word is always better than two. Let's get started. We have enough time to teach Sadie one more command today."

"Look it is."

For the next ten minutes, Derrick practiced gaining his dog's attention and rewarded her with a piece of kibble every time she looked up at him and held his gaze. Following Julie's instructions, he gradually delayed giving the reward until Sadie could sit and look for a full minute. She was a quick learner.

He hated to admit it, but apparently, their problems had stemmed from his lack of knowledge about communicating with a dog. Thanks to Julie's expertise, Melanie would have no complaints when she returned from her honeymoon in Hawaii. Derrick and Sadie would be a smoothly working team by that time. Their relationship had transformed from him providing shelter to creating a home for the loyal German shepherd. With a start, he realized that was on him, too. He'd expected her to be loyal and obedient without first earning her trust and winning her affection.

Julie glanced at the clock and back at him.

Five-thirty. His hour was up.

He could ask her to go for a burger, but she probably had another appointment coming in. He wanted to shake her hand and thank her for her help today, but she seemed to anticipate his intention and hugged her clipboard to her chest. He'd be a cad to ignore that body language. But he could still be charming. "Thank you, Julie. You're on your way to making Sadie one of your canine jewels."

She smiled, but her tired eyes made him wonder if she were working too hard, and if anyone helped her carry her load. He didn't think she employed any other trainers, and she hadn't mentioned a boyfriend. That recollection brought an instant smile to his lips. "You're a good teacher."

"I didn't do anything but provide you with time-proven training tips. You and Sadie did all the work."

He disagreed. "Someone should teach you how to accept a compliment, Julie Barnes. You are exceptionally good at what you do, and if it weren't for meeting you, I don't know where Sadie and I would be."

Her enchanting blue eyes shone with longing. But then she steeled her features into a professional mask that hid her feelings. "Thank you, Derrick. I'll see you on Tuesday at four-thirty."

Tuesday couldn't get here quick enough. He needed to figure out a way for their paths to cross before then.

He and Sadie weren't the only ones experiencing a growing connection. Julie felt it, too. And he wanted to find out where their mutual attraction might lead.

He could go to church on Sunday morning. He knew from her dad which church they attended, but Julie might suspect his motives. No. Going to church wasn't the way to get closer to Julie Barnes.

Not unless he intended to get closer to God first. And Derrick wasn't ready to make peace with God. After fifteen years, would he ever be?

Saturday morning, Julie was up by six. Needing to quiet her mind, she carried her first cup of coffee out to the back patio and sat on the chaise lounge. A cool breeze rustled the poplar leaves, and a squirrel scurried along the bough of a nearby maple. A mourning dove cooing high in a pine tree made Julie long for a similar peaceful confidence in God's provisions.

Decidedly unsettled, she wrapped her arms around her knees and struggled to pray. But her thoughts kept returning to her two perplexing problems. The farm and Derrick Walker. Both situations required clear direction from the Lord, and she was out of practice listening.

She sipped her coffee, savoring the hazelnut undertones. Stretching her legs, she adjusted the chaise to a more upright position, picked up her Bible from the end table, and thumbed through the pages until she reached the third chapter of Proverbs. Her grandmother had taught Julie and Jack to rely on verses five and six whenever life got confusing. She could still hear Grandma's sweet voice reading, "Trust in the LORD with all thine heart and lean not unto thine own understanding. In all thy ways acknowledge Him, and He shall direct thy paths."

"There are going to be times when you don't know what to do. That's the way life is." Grandma Barnes patted Jack's knee then caressed Julie's face, ensuring that both of her grandchildren were paying close attention. "But that's when you need to trust God the most. Because if you don't, Satan will tell you God doesn't care, and you don't want to believe his lies."

Julie sighed as the memory faded. They'd lost their grandmother in their teens, but that conversation meant more today than it had back then. How had twelve years passed so quickly?

Confident Grandma Barnes was happy in heaven, Julie took in the beautiful cumulus clouds, stunning against a perfect summer blue. "Grandma, I've met someone. His name is Derrick Walker. The sky today is the same glorious blue as his eyes. I think you'd like him. He's a good man."

She knew it was true, in spite of him being a cop.

No other man had filled the open spaces in her mind the way Derrick did. Even after Nick had proposed to her, she hadn't thought about him during every spare minute. Her attraction to Derrick was way over the top.

And she didn't know where he stood with God. If Derrick were an unbeliever, she would have to walk away from him.

As soon as she'd fulfilled his contract.

Humph. Contracts. The real estate agent had called again yesterday to set up an appointment for Julie to sign the contract to sell Shady Meadows. She couldn't continue to ignore the woman's calls.

"Lord, I need Your direction. I know You have good plans for me, but if keeping the farm and getting closer to Derrick aren't part of those plans, You are going to have to change my heart."

Taking a deep breath, she steeled herself for possible disappointment. "Because You already know I don't want to walk away from Shady Meadows or Derrick Walker."

Wait.

Wait? That was God's answer. She could wait. Waiting would be better than making the wrong decision. About Derrick or the farm.

On Saturday morning at nine-fifteen—more than 30 minutes later than she'd planned, Julie pulled into the church parking lot to drop off the promised cupcakes. She entered through the back door and hurried down the stairs and into the church kitchen, where several women were chatting as they worked to organize the baked goods. At the last minute, Julie had decided to pack the treats in two separate boxes, one labeled for sale and the other labeled for the pastor and his family. She handed the box designated for the pastor to Katie and set the other box on the counter.

With a wave that encompassed everyone, Julie said, "I'm heading out. Bye, ladies."

Katie thanked Julie for their box then whispered, "Are you going out to the farm?"

Julie nodded. "It's my Saturday routine."

"Have you made up your mind yet?"

"I think so."

After spending the day caring for the horses, Julie acknowledged she couldn't give them up. Not yet. On Monday, she would call Ms. Morrison and tell her she'd decided to wait to list the farm. Julie could make her decision by the end of the summer. People still bought property in the fall, right? A few more months wouldn't make much difference.

She would talk to her brother when he came home to visit next week. After all, her decision would impact him, too.

Shady Meadows had everything Derrick could need or want, including a three-car garage, two riding arenas, miles of riding trails, an apple orchard, a peach orchard, a large garden, various berries, and more than enough acreage to grow his own hay. The quaint farmhouse had two floors with a second-floor balcony across the front and at the ground-level, a wraparound veranda, featuring several groupings of lounge chairs, a table with seating for six people, and a porch swing equipped with comfortable cushions. Six hanging baskets filled with deep red geraniums and white and purple petunias invited hummingbirds and butterflies. This place was well worth giving up a Sunday afternoon lounging around with his dog or hanging out with Leon and Tamika and their kids.

Shady Meadows' spacious stables could house ten horses with ample length in the aisle between the stalls to set up three crossties. But Derrick planned on owning two or three horses at most. The six Paints and two Palominos curiously studying him from their well-kept stalls were more than he needed or wanted. "You're sure the owner will sell only if I agree to keep all of these horses?" He'd made no attempt to hide his frustration at what he considered to be a ridiculous and unrealistic condition.

Ms. Morrison's gaze shifted in every direction. "She did mention that."

Why wouldn't the woman look him in the eye? She was hiding something. But what? "Is there something else I need to know?" he asked, keeping his voice low and without accusation.

When the realtor faced him, her red face confirmed he'd caught her in some deception. Too bad. This was a great place, in good condition, better than he'd dreamed of finding, given the sacrifices some people had been forced to make in this area.

"Shady Meadows isn't exactly listed. Yet." Ms. Morrison straightened the collar of her blue suit.

He chalked this up to an unconscious, nervous gesture. She should be nervous. What she'd done may not be illegal, but it was certainly unethical and unprofessional.

"I see," he ground out.

But he didn't see at all. What was the point of dragging him all the way out here if the owner wasn't committed to selling?

"I assure you, Mr. Walker, the owner has every intention of selling." She nodded to emphasize the point.

But he didn't believe her.

Still, he listened patiently as the realtor elaborated on the many fine features of the fifty-acre farm. The place had been well-tended. Every building had been recently painted, probably in the last two or three years. The house and barn roofs were in excellent condition, which wasn't always the case with these old farms. He'd seen three in the past six months that would have required costly repairs beyond his budget, even with his Army benefits from the GI Bill.

Shady Meadows was everything he wanted. From the tire swing hanging in an old oak in the backyard to the wrap-around porch, every aspect of this place reminded him of his childhood home. The home they had lost when his parents had been killed by a drunk driver. Less than a week after the funeral, Derrick and Melanie had moved in with their maternal grandparents, to a three-bedroom city apartment with a shared backyard that wasn't big enough to toss a football back and forth with the guys.

Fifteen years later, he had enough money for a sizable down payment on a home where he could raise a family. If he ever found a woman who could accept that there were parts of his life he would never share with her. Things he didn't want to think about, much less talk about.

Julie's beautiful face popped unbidden into his head. He gave himself a mental slap. She could never be a part of his future, beyond the dog training sessions, nor did he suspect she wanted to be. Detective Barnes' daughter knew all too well what being married to a cop was like. She had watched her parents her whole life.

Be realistic, Walker. You want a relationship with her, but she's not the one, is she?

Returning his attention to the business at hand, Derrick informed the agent, "I've been looking for over a year. I haven't seen any place I like better than this. But I don't need all these horses. I'd be willing to keep the two Palominos and one Paint." He paused to let his next words carry the rebuke he believed the woman deserved. "Of course, this conversation and the two hours I've spent may turn out to be a total waste of my time."

To her credit, Ms. Morrison's face colored with chagrin. "You're right. I've never shown a client an unlisted property before. I ... apologize. Mr. Walker."

Derrick recognized her genuine remorse. "Forget it."

"Would you like me to contact you after the owner *has* signed the contract?"

He deliberately knit his brow into a disapproving frown. "What about the horses?"

Ms. Morrison's pensive expression indicated she was searching for a reasonable compromise. "If you match the seller's price, she may agree to let the place go with three of the horses."

He opened his mouth to argue, but the realtor put up her hand to interrupt him. "She'll want to sell the others herself to be sure they go to good homes, and she'll insist they remain here until then."

"That would work for me if Shady Meadows' current manager agrees to stay on at the seller's expense until the extra horses are sold. I might consider keeping him on myself. Part-time, of course." Derrick reached over to stroke the muzzle of a beautiful Palomino whose stall door proclaimed her name to be Sunny. Would the owner really accept his offer, together with the modification of her terms?

Provided she decided to sell.

It was a shame really. He'd fallen in love with a place that might never be his. "All right. Give me a call when you have a signed contract."

Ms. Morrison smiled, revealing perfectly capped teeth.

Probably purchased with her many commissions. Harsh cynicism. An unfortunate byproduct of years on the police force. "So, when do you think the owner will decide about selling? Not that I'm in any rush."

Ms. Morrison made a few notes in her planner. "I'll contact Ms. Barnes today when I return to my office. Then I'll phone you and let you know."

"*Julie* Barnes?"

A startled expression marred the agent's composed features. "You know Ms. Barnes?"

The blood rushed from his head. "She's helping me train my dog." He swallowed hard, drawing on years of training. Julie? This was her place. And she wanted to sell? He couldn't imagine why.

"Shall I call you after she's officially listed Shady Meadows?"

"That'd be great," he said, his mind scrambling for answers. Answers he could get only from Julie herself.

Derrick didn't shake the realtor's hand or bid her goodbye. He turned his back to her and walked away.

Sadie was waiting in the SUV parked in the shade of a towering maple tree. Curled up on the front seat, she looked completely relaxed, thanks to Julie's excellent advice. He could hardly wait to see Julie on Tuesday. She'd be happy with the progress they'd made.

He started the engine, closed the windows, and the

sunroof, then cranked up the air conditioner. He couldn't shake the feeling he was meant to see Julie's place. But why? His parents would have said his coming out here today was part of God's plan. Derrick shook his head. He didn't know what to believe. Could God have a plan for his life that included such minute details as what property he viewed in his search for a house?

Driving home, Derrick pondered two things. Why was Julie considering selling? And how would she feel about him being the buyer?

Maybe he should call off Ms. Morrison until he had time to discover how Julie felt about Shady Meadows. He could imagine her with a yellow lab at her feet, rocking on the porch swing, drinking lemonade and reading. What did she like to read? The Bible. She'd been reading it the other day at the park.

She was a Christian.

That was one more reason he was all wrong for her.

He hadn't prayed much, except in life or death situations. Not since his parents died. But Derrick remembered enough of his Sunday School lessons to know Julie would never consider dating an unbeliever.

He wasn't exactly an unbeliever. But he didn't have much faith or confidence in God's active participation in this world. After all, if God cared, his parents would still be alive and that drunk would have been sent to prison for DWI long before the old man plowed his pickup into Derrick's parents' Mustang convertible. The stupid little car had rolled over so many times that Mom and Dad were both dead at the scene before the paramedics arrived. Where had God been then? God couldn't possibly be in the minute details.

Chapter Five

It was eleven o'clock Monday morning before Julie found a minute to call the real estate agent. "Hello, Ms. Morrison, this is Julie Barnes. I apologize for not getting back to you sooner, but I've decided not to list Shady Meadows at this time."

"But ... but I may have a buyer," Ms. Morrison sputtered. "And he's made a solid offer."

Julie tapped her pen on her desk. Someone made a solid offer for the farm? How could that be when she hadn't agreed to list it? Because she couldn't trust this woman, that's why.

"Don't you at least want to hear the offer?"

"No. I'm sorry for the inconvenience to you, Ms. Morrison. And to the prospective buyer. But I need more time to consider my options."

"I see. You'll let me know if you change your mind?"

"Of course."

Julie hung up, drew in a deep breath, and let it out with a whoosh. She'd made the right decision. Her parents would be happy, and Jack would understand. Eventually.

Now, if God would only show her what to do about a certain charming cop, Julie's life would be stress-free.

Derrick and Sadie were heading out to pick up some lunch when his cell phone rang. Ms. Morrison explained that Julie had decided against selling the farm.

He wasn't surprised at all. He tamped down his annoyance and disappointment. "I understand. Thank you for calling."

He abruptly disconnected the call before the realtor could draw him into a conversation. He had no intention of working with her in the future. He would have to find a new agent to continue his search.

Shady Meadows was the perfect place for him, and although it wasn't meant to be, he couldn't help thinking Melanie would've loved having her own horse again. When they'd had to sell their home years ago to pay off their parents' debts, his teenage sister hadn't uttered a word of complaint, but giving up her afternoon trail rides on her beloved Misty, was hard for Mel. And hard for him, too, because he hadn't been able to come up with another solution.

But things were different now. He was a grown man with resources and options. Having horses again would be good for him, too, but he'd had a hunch when he first learned Shady Meadows belonged to Julie that she didn't really want to sell. But why had she considered listing it in the first place? She didn't seem like the indecisive type who changed her plans on a whim.

Walker, you're thinking about this woman way too much. It's time you came clean and asked her out.

He raked his hand through his hair. Had he admitted he wanted to ask Julie out in spite of all the reasons he shouldn't? Especially considering their spiritual differences.

Apparently tuned in to his mood, Sadie cocked her head at him, and he reached across the console to rub the dog's head between her ears. "What do you think, girl? Will the lady say yes?"

Sadie barked three times.

Derrick chuckled and decided to ignore the nagging thought that Julie's answer might be no and to listen to his dog. "I'll take that as a yes, girl."

He shrugged. After all, he was only asking Julie to have lunch with him. As friends.

Yeah, right. Who are you kidding?

His conscience stabbed at him, too.

"What do You expect me to do, God? I can't get her out of my head."

His mother always said God demanded honesty.

Well, Derrick was being honest. About his feelings for Julie. As for the rest, he'd figure that out later.

A quick glance at the dash display told him it was nearly noon. He could meet up with Julie at the park. He suspected she liked a regular routine, and the weather was perfect for a picnic lunch, sunny with a nice breeze. He parked on Main Street and stopped at the bakery first. Not knowing what she would prefer, he opted for chocolate cream cheese brownies. He hadn't met a woman yet who didn't like chocolate.

Deciding to walk to the deli, he opened the sunroof and the windows several inches to keep the car cool for Sadie. He patted her head and promised to return in a few minutes. Then he exited the car, locked the doors, and pulled his cell phone out to call Julie.

She answered on the first ring. "Hello, Julie's Canine Jewels. How may I help you?"

"You can have lunch with me."

"Derrick, is everything all right? How are you? How are things going with Sadie?"

"Like the difference between the mountains and the desert."

"Huh?"

"Okay, like night and day, all right? My mother hated clichés. She insisted we make up our own comparisons."

"Oh, so she was a teacher?"

"No, she was a children's writer. But I didn't call you to talk about my mother. Would you like to have lunch with me today? I've already got dessert. I'm heading to the deli now so if you'll tell me which sandwich you want ..."

Her long pause made him wonder if their call had been dropped.

"My favorite is pastrami on rye loaded with spicy mustard, and fresh deli pickles on the side."

The smile in her voice made something shift inside of him. Maybe God did care about the details. Julie had agreed to lunch. It was a start.

I won't hurt her, God. I promise You that.

Derrick shook his head at himself. Was he on speaking terms with God again?

"Derrick? Did I lose you?"

"No, Julie. Sorry. I'm here."

"Make sure you get chips."

He suggested he pick her up, but she said she had errands to do after lunch. They arranged to meet at the park in fifteen minutes. He arrived before Julie, so he decided to give Mel a fast call. As usual, his sister's skills in reading him far exceeded his abilities to conceal anything from her. She should have been a lawyer, rather than an advertiser.

"You met someone."

"Whatever gave you such a crazy idea?"

"Don't you dare try that cop nonsense on me. You haven't sounded this happy in ... I don't know how long. You have definitely met someone."

In the background, Bob was laughing. "No way,

Mel."

"He did, Bob, I know he did."

Derrick absently stroked Sadie's fur and handed her a dog biscuit, which she took without even grazing his fingers with her teeth. "Aren't you going to ask me how Sadie and I are getting along?"

"Well, of course. But don't think I don't know what you're doing, trying to throw me off track. How is my dog?"

"*My* dog and I are getting along great, thanks to a certain curly-haired blonde."

"What? You mean Julie Barnes?"

"That would be her. She's an excellent, intuitive trainer. Julie's worked wonders with Sadie and me." He hooked a four-foot lead to Sadie's collar then staked the lead under a maple tree in sight of a nearby picnic table.

Car tires crunching gravel alerted him to an approaching vehicle. He spotted Julie in her beat-up Ford. "Listen, Sis, Julie's here. I'll call you in a few days."

"Julie Barnes is the woman you're seeing?"

"We're having lunch, not planning an engagement party, okay?"

"Very funny. Can I help it if I want my big brother to be deliriously happy?"

He shook his head at his sister reversing roles and trying to watch out for him. "I appreciate your concern, but I am happy. I'll call you soon. Bye." He ended the call before his sister could ask anymore nosy questions.

Eager to begin their first date, Derrick hurried across the grass to meet the woman who had filled his imagination for the past week. Wearing a long, blue cotton skirt that accented her legs when the wind caught the light fabric and a white peasant blouse with flowers embroidered around the collar and cuffs, she was stunning.

Sadie barked a greeting, and Julie waved, beaming at both him and his dog.

Immensely glad he'd won her approval, Derrick closed the distance between them. Their eyes met, and he wanted to wrap his arms around her and pull her close. This spark between them didn't make any sense but couldn't be denied. Before he could overthink it, he leaned in and kissed her flushed cheek, letting his lips linger on her smooth satin skin. Her floral perfume wafted to his nose and stirred his already heightened senses. He stepped back to regain his equilibrium. "You look beautiful."

Her hand covered her cheek where he had kissed it, but anxiety marred her beautiful eyes.

His protective instincts roared to life. Derrick fought the urge to sweep Julie into his arms and reassure her that his being a cop wouldn't matter, shouldn't matter. They'd figure it out. But he couldn't say any of that. Not yet. Not when she was fighting her attraction to him.

He wasn't in the habit of overlooking reality. Face all obstacles, head-on whenever possible, unless the situation demanded retreat.

But retreating was no longer an option because she'd already captured his heart.

Julie frowned at him, then averted her face. "I think you may have misunderstood. I don't date ... clients."

How could he respond to that? Stalling, he glanced over at Sadie, who was resting in the shade of the massive maple tree. The shepherd cocked her head and barked twice as if to say, you better be straight with Julie. Derrick shook his head. Now, he was imagining two-way conversations with his dog.

Okay, God, if You really care the way my parents always said You did, help me now. Julie isn't like any other woman I've ever met. She's special and smart. And You know I think she's beautiful. And I ...

Her hand on his arm broke into his prayer. Prayer? When exactly had he started praying again? When he'd fallen for a Christian woman. That's when.

"Derrick, are you all right?"

"I'm fine." Encouraged by her concern, he decided to be completely honest. "I asked you to have lunch with me because I'd like to get to know you better." *Because I think I'm falling in love with you.*

But he couldn't tell her that. Not yet away.

She was silent. Why didn't she say something? He tried to get a read on her reaction. Her demeanor was thoughtful. Maybe, a bit fearful. Had he made his move too soon? Would she turn him down cold? He steeled himself for her refusal.

But she smiled. "As long as you remember we can't

be more than friends."

Because you don't date cops, clients, or backsliders.

Derrick couldn't do anything about the first point, but he wouldn't always be her client. And as for being a backslider—that obstacle he could remove. If he were willing to let go of his anger and bitterness. Was he? Could he do that for her? It wouldn't be easy. Or instant. But Julie was worth it.

"I can do friendship." He wanted to add that some of the best romances began with friendship, but he didn't dare push his luck.

She smiled again. "Let's eat. I'm starving."

Together, they walked to the picnic table, and he unpacked their lunch. Julie pulled three chilled bottles of water from her canvas bag and poured one into Sadie's bowl while he laid out the food. For a few minutes, they ate in silence until she asked him how he and Sadie were getting along. Julie made a few workable suggestions to tweak his training.

By the time they got to dessert, he and Julie were talking like two people getting acquainted on a first date, though she'd claimed this wasn't a date. Before he realized where the conversation was headed, they were discussing their childhoods. Not ready to talk about his parents, Derrick asked her what she did as a kid for fun. They had far more in common than he had imagined. She scoffed when he admitted to enjoying board games, until he confessed that Clue was his favorite. He waited to see if she'd ask about him wanting to be a cop, even as a kid, but she either didn't make the connection or she didn't want to start an argument. He changed the subject to favorite outdoor activities and brought up his love of horses and the country. She said she'd loved riding since she was a little girl. He almost asked her about Shady Meadows, but he didn't want to ruin the mood.

Julie considered asking Derrick about his faith, or the lack of it. From the way he'd described his parents, they'd been Christians, which made Derrick's silence on the subject perplexing. But asking him wouldn't alleviate her anxiety. A man could say anything he wanted. She needed visible proof. She'd learned that from Nick.

Deciding to avoid the topic of religion, she asked Derrick about his military service. He told her about how awful boot camp had been but said nothing about his time in a combat zone.

She didn't want to imagine the things he'd experienced. The things he'd had to do. "Did you join the Army because you really believe freedom is not free?"

He was silent for a long moment, and the pain in his eyes was almost more than she could bear.

Until the unbreachable mask slipped into place, concealing his thoughts. He shook his head. "Not exactly."

"You *weren't* inspired by your patriotism?"

"Julie, I don't expect you to understand."

Noting his frustration, she decided not to press him. "If you don't want to talk about it, I get it."

He shrugged. "Okay, I'll tell you how it was. Like so many guys, my idea of heroism was formed by the romanticized images of the military I'd seen in the movies, read in books, watched on the news. Basically, I enlisted because of teenaged ideals about glory."

He paused, and his eyes reflected his painful past. As she waited for him to continue or to change the subject, anxiety skittered from her tight throat to her clenched stomach.

He averted his face then shot her an earnest look, an obvious plea for her understanding. She started to tell him she could see how the pursuit of glory could motivate a young guy to enlist.

But Derrick shook his head to silence her. "Don't get me wrong. I'm proud to have served my country. But once you get over there, war isn't about politics or patriotism. All you really think about is making it back home."

Making it back home? Of course, he'd thought about that. Because he might not. She reached for his hands, and he clasped hers in return as if she were his lifeline. She could comfort him as a friend, couldn't she?

His expression changed, like a wall going up between them. His dark brows knit together in a deep frown, and he abruptly pulled his hands free, grabbed his half-empty water bottle, and strode over to Sadie as if he couldn't get away from Julie fast enough. She blinked back tears as Derrick dumped the rest of his water in the dog's stainless-steel bowl, stroked Sadie's head, and plodded back to the picnic table.

Julie considered changing the subject, but before she could say anything, Derrick gave her a sad smile.

"I started bootcamp when I was twenty. Right after I got Melanie settled at the Pittsburgh Art Institute." He scrunched his empty chip bag into a ball and wadded up his napkin together with the paper his sandwich had been wrapped in. His eyes briefly met hers. "That was three years after our parents died."

Shock stole her breath, and her hands flew to her mouth then settled, restless on the table. She couldn't imagine that kind of pain. She'd lived with the fear of losing her dad, but this was far worse. "You lost both your parents at the same time? How?"

"It was a car accident. They were both killed instantly. I was seventeen. Melanie had celebrated her fifteenth birthday the week before."

For a moment, the grief ravaging his face transformed this strong, confident man into someone she didn't recognize, into a heartbroken teen forced to grow up in a single day.

Julie wanted to wrap her arms around him, to absorb some his grief, but instead, she reached across the table and enclosed his hands. His fingers were cold, and she wriggled her hands free and started to rub his hands to warm them. Was she crossing a line she shouldn't breach with this man? No, she was simply letting him know he could share as much or as little as he wanted. She was letting him know she cared. Friends cared.

Derrick raised his gaze from their hands, and the conflicting emotions in his eyes reflected her own.

"You're special, Julie Barnes." He caressed her face with his gaze. "Why am I telling you stuff I haven't talked about in years?"

A couple of ideas came to her mind, neither of which Julie was willing to reveal. Yet. But he looked so disappointed that she blurted out the truth. "Maybe because you feel safe with me."

"Safe? It's my job as a cop to make sure *you* are safe."

Her heart lurched, and she snatched her hands away from his and hid them in her lap. Cops were never safe. She had no idea how often his life was in danger. Daily? Weekly? How could she have forgotten that fact?

Why had she agreed to have lunch with him? She couldn't just be friends with Derrick. Not now. All they'd shared today had taken their relationship way beyond professional, and her attraction to him had grown exponentially. Tears pricked her eyes, threatening to fall. She had to get away.

"I'm sorry, Derrick, but I need to get back." She glanced quickly at her watch—a gesture to support her feeble excuse. "I have an appointment in twenty minutes."

Before he could respond, or question her abruptness, she leapt to her feet, grabbed her purse, and ran across the freshly cut grass toward her car.

But she didn't get far.

With his hand on her arm, Derrick gently turned her to face him. "Julie, I—"

"Please, I need to go."

He released her, and she backed up several steps to put more distance between them. She couldn't face him, so she stared at her feet.

"Listen, Julie. I know you weren't talking about physical safety. Sometimes my mouth kicks into gear before my brain. Bringing up the cop thing was totally insensitive."

Why did she have to like him so much? She swallowed around the tight pain in her throat. She refused to cry. Tears never changed anything.

I put your tears in a bottle.

Julie stilled at God's gentle reminder of His total love for her. But she and Derrick could never work. She raised her face to his. Nearly undone by the earnest hope in his eyes, she said, "You didn't do anything wrong. You're a cop. We both forgot that."

"Please, don't leave, Julie. Not yet. We have to talk about this."

"I'm sorry, Derrick." She rested her hand on his upper arm then drew back, not wanting to give him the wrong message. "I'll see you and Sadie at your *scheduled* appointment tomorrow afternoon at four-thirty."

Despite the sorrow in her tone, her emphasis on the word scheduled reinforced her point.

He nodded.

But the hurt in his eyes was a knife in her stomach.

"Of course. I don't want to make you late."

She trudged the rest of the way to her car as if the soles of her shoes were made of lead. Derrick's gaze pulled her like a magnet drawing her to his side.

Lunch had been a mistake.

Derrick stared at Julie as she climbed into her car. He willed her to stay, but the Ford's engine roared to life, and she backed out onto the road heading out of the park. He had made a stupid mistake. He'd spoiled their time together by reminding her he was a cop.

He'd always be a cop. The risks in his occupation created problems anyone involved with a police officer would face daily. Julie dealt with those problems now with her dad. She didn't want to face them with the man she married. But she wouldn't even date him unless she believed he was marriage material. Derrick understood that much from their conversation over lunch. Choosing not to date casually was something they had in common.

He wouldn't *be* marriage material unless he made

things right between himself and God.

Julie's car disappeared over the hill, and Derrick's thoughts drifted back to his sister's wedding day. She'd kissed his cheek and whispered, "One day, you're going to meet the woman God's meant for you. Then, you're going to be as happy as Bob and I."

Melanie would probably say Julie was that woman.

Frustrated with himself, Derrick cleaned up the picnic area. He tucked the water bottles into the empty brown bag so he could recycle them later and dumped everything else in the trash.

Sadie gave a short bark to gain his attention. When he reached her, she licked the back of his hand. To think he'd almost missed this amazing relationship. He bent to kiss the top of her head. "I love you, Sadie girl. You're a good dog."

Sadie planted a slobbery kiss on his cheek.

Derrick yanked out the stake, disconnected it from Sadie's lead, and together he and his dog headed to his SUV. The minute he opened the passenger door, Sadie scrambled up onto the front seat. He settled into the driver's side and turned his key in the ignition to get the air conditioner going. "Let's go home, girl. It's time for me to deal with some old issues, and then, come up with a plan to fix things with Julie."

Sadie nuzzled his hand.

He gazed into his dog's loving eyes and stroked her head. "Thanks for the vote of confidence, girl."

Too bad Julie didn't trust him as much as Sadie did.

The irony of that thought made hope surge through his veins. Smiling, Derrick shifted the SUV into gear, determined to get his life back on the right track.

Twenty minutes later, he pulled up to his ranch house, intending to work out lifting weights for an hour or so, but his grass needed cutting, badly. Last night's hard rain had made the difference. He took Sadie in the house, gave her some water, and considered letting her have free rein in the house while he worked outside.

With dark eyes twinkling, the shepherd cocked her head, and wagged her tail as if she'd read his mind. "I don't think so, girl. Not yet." He headed into the kitchen with Sadie following on his heels. "Go crate."

Sadie obeyed. She circled her crate once then curled up onto her soft, clean blanket.

"Good girl. I won't be long."

He locked the crate, grabbed a bottled water from the fridge, and headed outside to tackle the lawn. Walking behind the mower was a mindless task, which was okay. He had a lot of thinking to do.

He cut the spacious backyard first, all the while forcing himself to return to that horrible night and the awful days that followed. The grief he'd denied for years erupted like water rushing through a breached dam, but the whirr of the mower muffled his sobs.

By the time, he'd finished cutting the backyard and started on the front, Derrick had examined the impact of his self-appointed role as Melanie's protector. His vow to shield his sister from as much pain as possible had made sense at the time. But that had meant burying his own feelings. And never letting Mel see how his grief and anger eroded his faith and sent him careening into a dark place where he rejected God. The God who had let his parents die at the hands of a low-life, scumbag drunk didn't deserve Derrick's worship. He'd refused to serve such a God.

Even though she was two years younger than he was, Melanie had chosen to deal with her grief. She'd run to God, rather than running from Him. She'd cried for months until one day she accepted the tragic loss of their parents and moved forward, transformed into a person who embraced possibilities.

But Derrick didn't let God transform *him*, and because he couldn't transform himself, he became adept at wearing the mask of a young man who appeared to walk with the Lord, who attended church every week with his family, but who never entered into the blessings others received with unfettered joy and thanksgiving.

Derrick had paid a hefty price for his stubborn rejection of God's grace, one he couldn't have anticipated. Deceiving his sister had hardened him, and the easy camaraderie they'd shared before their parents' deaths was gone.

Once he'd started boot camp, the need for duplicity had ended. He'd believed himself home-free, confident his spiritual desolation couldn't possibly hurt his sister anymore. But he'd been wrong.

Derrick made the final pass in the front yard, parked the mower in the garage, and hauled out the weed-whacker. As he methodically trimmed around the trees and shrubs, he let himself remember the day he found out Melanie knew what he'd become.

They were saying goodbye outside her dormitory. One minute, she was giggling, excited and happy to be starting college. The next minute, she threw her arms around his neck and started sobbing. He couldn't imagine why she was crying. She'd been looking forward to studying photography, to developing her talent for taking photos that captured the essence and soul of her subjects. And now she was crying so hard people were staring at them.

"Mel, talk to me. What's wrong?"

Placing her hands on each side of his face, his sister forced him to hold her heartbroken gaze. "It wasn't God's fault, Derrick. Every day, I pray you'll finally see that. How much longer are you going to make me wait for the answer to my prayers?"

Her anguished face seared his heart and mind. What could he say? He'd failed to protect her because he'd chosen to reject the God she continued to serve.

He took her hands in his. Her trembling unnerved him more than her words. "I'll try, Melanie. That's all I can do. I promise you I'll try to find my way back."

But Derrick hadn't kept that promise. He'd shut God out completely, rationalizing His blessings, calling them good luck, rather than God's goodness. In the process, he'd forged a bigger wedge between himself and the Lord.

And now, his bitterness threatened to hurt another woman he loved. He would lose any chance with Julie if he didn't set things right. But how? How could he undo the damage he'd done?

Derrick raked the chopped weeds into piles, scooped all the refuse into a garbage bag, and put the rake and weed-whacker away. The yard looked great, so he headed into the house to let Sadie out in the backyard.

She greeted him with a happy bark, and when he opened the crate, she licked his hand. Following Julie's advice had totally transformed his relationship with his dog. How strange that he and Julie hadn't known each other for two weeks yet. He couldn't imagine not having her in his life.

Sadie scampered to the back door, and Derrick followed. "Let's go outside, girl. You need a chance to run."

After twenty minutes of playing catch using a lacrosse ball, Sadie finally plopped down in a shady spot under the grape arbor and promptly fell asleep.

Envying the shepherd's contentment, Derrick reclined on a patio lounge chair. It was time for him to do some serious praying.

If arguing with God could be called praying. He wasn't sure how long it took, but eventually Derrick reached the end of his questions and accusations. He slipped off the comfortable chair and onto his knees on the hard, cold flagstone.

Lord, You know I've blamed You for Mom and Dad dying. You know I've been angry because You had the power to save them and You didn't. I still don't understand why You didn't prevent the accident, but I'm ready to let go of my bitterness. I don't want to be angry at You anymore. I'm sorry it took me so long. Please, forgive me. Answer my sister's prayers. She's waited long enough already.

There on his knees in his backyard, Derrick felt scrubbed clean to the depth of his soul. How he'd missed the peace that comes from having nothing between him and the Lord. His parents had walked in that same peace. And now they walked with the Lord in heaven. Derrick wouldn't call them back here, even if he could. They were enjoying the rewards of their life-long service.

His own service for the Lord had been interrupted for more than fifteen years. He couldn't change the past, but the present and the future would be blessed, and he would honor the Giver of those blessings. Derrick didn't know if Julie would be a part of his future, but he believed God cared about the man she would marry.

Lord willing, Derrick wanted to be that man.

By the time he was showered and dressed for work, he had formulated a plan. Step one, ask Leon Martin for advice. His partner was not only happily married with three adorable daughters, he also took his family to church faithfully every Sunday. Leon had courted his wife, Tamika, who had resisted his early attempts to get to know her. Leon would gladly share how he'd won Tamika's heart.

Derrick wasn't usually a patient man, but he was determined to do whatever was necessary to win Julie's heart.

Julie managed to keep thoughts of Derrick at bay until the last client and his rambunctious chocolate lab bounded out the front door. At five-thirty, she collapsed on the sofa in the reception area and permitted herself a moment to consider what exactly had happened between her and Derrick at the park.

He'd opened up to her about his parents' deaths, and in exchange, she'd unwittingly given him a piece of her heart. How could she have let that happen? Friendship was out of the question for them. The feel of his hands enclosing hers was imprinted permanently on her heart.

No. That couldn't be.

Her heart had nothing to do with what had happened between them. It was a simple attraction. Nothing more.

Derrick was an attractive man. Any healthy woman would be drawn to him.

But he wasn't a Christian. She knew that now.

With Nick, Julie had wanted so badly to believe he

shared her faith that her own hopes and desires had made it easy for him to deceive her. He'd sat beside her in church, sang hymns, read the Bible, and pretended to be what he was not. She'd been so gullible and naïve. When he'd started pressuring her to abandon her promise to wait until marriage to share a physical relationship, she'd made excuses for him. Until the day she'd found him with another girl. Nick's betrayal had broken her heart and shattered her faith in herself.

Lord, I've forgiven Nick. And I think I've forgiven myself for not seeking Your guidance from the moment I first saw him. Now, I need You to help me set up boundaries between myself and Derrick. I want to safeguard my heart for the man You have intended for me.

She drew in a deep calming breath. She hugged her knees to her chest and ignored the single tear sliding down her cheek. After Sadie completed her lessons, Julie wouldn't see Derrick again. Never again would she put her interest in any man before her commitment to the Lord. No matter how much she cared for Derrick. No matter how much he seemed to care for her. Even if she could deal with the stress of being married to a cop.

She and Derrick would go their separate ways.

Chapter Six

Unless Derrick could change Julie's mind about dating a cop, they'd be going their separate ways in less than three weeks. He couldn't let that happen.

Lord, I'm counting on Leon to help me formulate a plan to win Julie's hand. Give us wisdom and show me the way, please.

Leon and Derrick were three hours into their shift before he had a chance to broach the subject. They were parked at a Tim Horton's, drinking their first coffees of the night when Derrick asked, "You're happily married, right, Leon?"

"Happier than I deserve to be, man. Tamika's the best."

Unlike many men Derrick knew, his partner had never uttered a single complaint about his wife.

Whenever Derrick had seen them socially, he'd been impressed with the respect, consideration, and genuine affection the couple shared. That's what marriage should be. And could be for Derrick and Julie. If he could move her past the friendship stage.

"Leon, how long did you and Tamika know each other before you asked her out?"

Hoping to conceal how badly he wanted his partner's input, Derrick stared into his coffee cup, but pretending to be casually unconcerned was a waste of time. Leon's gaze bored into him. Not surprising. Never once in the five years they'd been partners had Derrick ever brought up marriage or dating. Not to mention the fact they'd become experts at reading each other.

Three years ago, Tamika and Leon had sprung a surprise blind date on Derrick. Partners couldn't avoid talking to each other, but for about a week after that dating fiasco, conversation between them dwindled to essential information. Until Derrick finally wised up and realized that Tamika, a typical romantic female, wanted everyone to be as happy as she and Leon were. At the time, Derrick hadn't been ready to share his life with anyone. But he'd forgiven Leon and Tamika for their well-intentioned matchmaking.

"Why exactly do you want to know this now?"

Derrick slanted a look at his partner. "I've met someone."

Leon laughed, choked, and sprayed coffee from his gaping mouth. "*You*? You met someone? Mister The-girl-for-me-doesn't-exist?"

The older man wasn't making this easy. Didn't he realize Derrick needed advice? "Yes, I've met someone. She's the trainer who's been helping me with my sister's dog. At first, I didn't think I could work with the woman, and now, I can't stop thinking about her." Derrick turned on the ignition and made a right turn out of the parking lot. This conversation had to be easier without the pressure of making regular eye contact.

"So, what's the big deal? Lord knows, you're out of practice, Walker, but all you have to do is call her and ask her out."

Derrick rested one hand on the top of the steering wheel and with the other raked his fingers through his hair. He still hadn't gotten it cut. "It's not that simple."

"So, it's complicated. Why exactly?"

Derrick flipped on the flashing light and careened left to follow a speeding BMW. "Her name's Julie Barnes."

"You don't mean she's—"

"Yep, she's Detective Barnes' daughter."

"That is a problem. I take it she doesn't date cops."

Derrick nodded. "I tried arranging a spontaneous lunch at the park this afternoon. All I did was kiss her hello on the cheek, and she freaked. Said she doesn't date clients."

"Clients?"

"Yeah, remember. I told you. She's the dog trainer

my sister recommended for Sadie."

"That *is* complicated. My advice is to take it real slow. Get to know her while you're working with the dog. Show her she can trust you."

The driver of the BMW picked up speed. Forty-seven in a thirty-five. Didn't this guy see the flashing lights? Derrick turned on the siren. One block. Two blocks. Three blocks.

The owner of the BMW glanced up at his rear-view mirror then eased his car onto the rough shoulder. Who knew when Buffalo would have the money to fix the streets in this section of the city? Derrick pulled in behind the man, who appeared to be in his sixties, Caucasian, white hair. Some canned elevator music was blasting from his radio. Didn't the guy know he should shut the thing off? Or at least turn it down enough so he could hear a siren blaring behind him?

"You want to write this bozo a ticket, or should I?" Leon asked.

"I got it." Derrick exited the squad car, strode to the silver BMW, and tapped on the guy's window. A second after the suspect lowered the window, the odor of stale whiskey assaulted Derrick's nostrils. They were dealing with at least a DUI, if not a DWI. The guy blew willingly in the Breathalyzer. One point two percent. They'd have to take the bozo to the station. What a way to start a Monday night.

❀

The following morning, the aroma of bacon frying woke Julie. Jack was home. She stumbled out of bed, retrieved her summer bathrobe from the closet, stuffed her feet into flip-flop slippers, and hurried down the stairs.

From the kitchen doorway, she spotted her dad buttering toast while her mom scrambled eggs and cheese in a deep skillet. Her brother was turning over strips of crackling bacon and humming a tune he'd probably made up himself. "You're home early."

Jack held out his arms, and Julie squeezed him in her strongest bear hug.

"I missed you, Jewels."

"I missed you, too." More than a brother to her, Jack was a friend she could count on. If only he didn't have to stay away so long. Law school kept him mega busy. The third year was worse than the first two. In addition to his course load, he was writing for the law review. They hadn't seen him since Aunt Elaine's funeral in mid-January, and he'd only stayed two days.

Jack gently set her from him. "Let me look at you." He scrutinized her from head to toe. "Mom's right. You have lost weight. And those frown lines are back between your eyebrows. What's up, Jewels?"

Stalling, she walked to the counter, poured a mug of coffee, stirred in chocolate creamer, and took a long swallow of the mocha brew to gather her thoughts. No way did she want to have this discussion with their parents present. "Nothing, except ..." She looked from her brother to her dad to her mom. Their eyes told it all. "Mom already told you, didn't she, Jack?" Annoyed by her mother's interference, Julie whirled to face her. "That's great, Mom. Why didn't you—"

"Don't be mad at Mom." Jack laid his hand on Julie's arm. "I asked her to fill me in."

Julie set her mug on the table with a thump, and coffee sloshed over the rim, leaving a puddle on the vinyl tablecloth. "What exactly did she tell you?"

"Only that you'd seen a realtor," Mom interrupted, "but that you haven't listed Shady Meadows yet."

Dad handed Mom a plate with two slices of toast. "Let's fix our plates, honey, and have breakfast on the porch, so Julie and Jack can talk things over."

Mom pursed her lips together, then nodded, and in a few minutes, she and Dad left Julie alone with her brother.

Discouraged, she mopped up the spilled coffee with a napkin and topped off her mug. "I didn't list the farm because I was waiting to talk it over with you."

Jack's brows furrowed in genuine confusion. "Why would you consider selling? Aunt Elaine left Shady Meadows to you. It was what she and Uncle Fred planned when they drew up a new will three years ago."

"Why would they do that? How is that fair to you? Or to Mom?"

"Oh, so that's it." Jack lifted the last of the bacon out of the frying pan and laid it on paper towels to drain the excess fat. "Mom didn't explain their reasons to you."

"What are you talking about? Whose reasons?"

He gestured for her to sit. "We'll talk over breakfast. I'm starving."

"You're always starving."

"For somebody who has abundant patience with dogs, you're pretty impatient with people."

She swatted her brother with the nearest dish towel.

He shot her a wounded look. "Seriously? You still can't take constructive criticism?"

She laughed. "Fair enough, Jack."

He grinned triumphantly. "You never could best me in an argument."

"Which is why you're going to be an excellent lawyer."

He took a bow, flourishing his right arm like a Shakespearean actor. Then, he piled scrambled eggs and crispy bacon onto a platter and set it on the table next to a plate stacked with whole wheat toast. After retrieving cherry preserves and blueberry jam from the refrigerator, Jack chose the chair across from her. He led her in a short prayer to thank God for the food.

"Okay, spill it."

Jack snagged four slices of bacon and dumped a pile of eggs onto his plate. "I'm surprised Mom didn't tell you herself. She doesn't usually hold anything back."

"She tried talking to me," Julie said as she filled her own plate. Mentally adding up the calories, she decided she'd need to run tonight. "You know how she is, Jack. If I opened up the conversation, she'd tell me what *she* wanted me to do, and I needed to make my own decision. One I can live with."

Jack popped a whole slice of bacon into his mouth and chewed. "From where I sit, the decision's already been made for you. You only have to accept it."

"I'm starting to think everybody knows something I don't know. If there's a story to tell, I want to hear it from you, Jack."

"It's pretty simple." He leaned across the table to make his point. "I got Yale, and you get Shady Meadows."

She placed a scoop of eggs and two slices of bacon on a piece of toast and folded it into a sandwich. "I don't understand."

Mom appeared in the kitchen doorway. "Understand what? Haven't you told her yet?"

"I told her," Jack said. "But Jewels doesn't understand why Aunt Elaine left Shady Meadows to her and not to you."

"I would have thought it was obvious." Mom laid her hand on Julie's shoulder, pausing to make sure she was listening. "Your aunt couldn't have children of her own. That's why she left you Shady Meadows. To Fred and Elaine, you and Jack were more like a daughter and a son than a niece and a nephew. And that was okay with me and your dad. Sharing you and your brother was a gift we could give my baby sister and her husband. Your father and I agreed you and Jack should spend as much time on the farm as possible, especially in the summers."

Julie let what her mother was saying settle in her head. "I never knew." She searched her brother's face. "Did you?"

"Not when we were kids, no."

Mom pulled up a chair and sat next to Julie. "Your father thought it would be good for both of you to get away from the stress of worrying about him all the time. And, of course, of seeing him at his worst, when he'd say things to us he didn't mean."

"It wasn't that bad, Mom," Jack said, slathering cherry preserves on his third piece of toast. "Dad was a little grouchy sometimes, but I always figured he was upset about something that happened at work. Something he couldn't and wouldn't want to tell us about. I never took his bad moods personally."

What could Julie say to that? How had Jack, at three years younger than she, have figured all that out? She had always known their father loved them, but she didn't understand him. Sometimes, he seemed like two people to her. Which was what Jack was saying. Wasn't it? She longed to give Derrick a chance, but she couldn't, wouldn't get close to a man who acted like two people. Never knowing whether he would be cross or tender with her. She couldn't live like that. But it didn't matter anymore. She'd promised the Lord she wouldn't get involved with an unbeliever again. And she'd as much as told Derrick they needed to keep things professional.

It shouldn't be that difficult to corral her feelings. She'd known Derrick for less than two weeks, and she didn't believe in love at first sight. Chemistry at first sight, definitely. But not love. And wanting to be loved wasn't the same thing as being in love. Dating Nick had taught her that lesson, too.

Forcing herself to focus on the matter at hand, she searched her mom's eyes for the truth. "I still don't see how it's fair for me to get the farm."

Mom glanced at her watch. "Honey, we both need to get to work, so I'm going to give you the condensed version. When Elaine got her cancer diagnosis, she changed her will, leaving everything to you. She knew your brother didn't want the farm—not with his plans to be a prominent lawyer."

Jack grinned at the praise. In less than a year, he would graduate from Yale Law School. Her brother had plans to live in D.C., where he believed he could do the most good. "Thanks for the vote of confidence, Mom. I'm glad you think they made a good investment."

"Investment?" Julie asked.

"Your aunt and uncle paid for Jack's law school," Mom said.

"What? Seriously? *That's* what you meant when you said you got Yale?"

Caught with a mouthful of toast, Jack nodded.

"Your dad and I saved only enough money for each of you to attend college for four years," Mom explained.

"When Elaine and Fred found out we didn't have enough for law school, they promised to pay for Jack to go wherever he wanted. He chose Yale."

Stunned, Julie couldn't believe what she was hearing. But it was exactly the kind of thing Aunt Elaine and Uncle Fred would do.

"It was their gift to your brother," Mom explained. "And Shady Meadows was her gift to you, Julie. Because she knew you loved the farm as much as she did."

Julie couldn't speak. Words she wanted to say tangled around the sobs building in her throat. Sobs she didn't dare release. She didn't have to sell the farm? Or the horses? She swallowed hard. She couldn't cry, because if she started, she didn't know if she could stop.

Mom covered Julie's trembling hand with her steady one. "Honey, broken hearts don't heal unless we let the tears out."

Julie shook her head. Tears had never healed her heart before. And tears definitely didn't bring back those she loved. So, she'd been determined to simply buckle up and endure. Endure the pain like a good soldier until things got better. Or until she could distract herself with work. Would it be better to cry it all out?

"When my sister told me she'd decided to leave the farm to you, the joy on her face lit up the whole room like Main Street at Christmas. She was so happy talking about how you could have your dog school out in the country with plenty of room to expand. She wanted to give you the freedom to explore whatever dreams God placed in your heart."

"I wish she'd told me." Tears slid in rivulets down Julie's cheeks. "So I could've thanked her."

"I know, honey. She'd planned to tell you." Momentary sadness flitted across Mom's face, but she composed herself, rose from the table, and bent to kiss Julie's wet cheek. "She knew how much you loved her."

Julie wiped her face with a napkin. "I miss her, Mom."

"I do, too, honey. But she would want us to be happy."

Jack nodded his agreement, and Julie smiled.

Mom opened the refrigerator door and grabbed the lunch she'd packed the night before. "I have to be in my car in five minutes to get to work on time. Jack, tell your sister she has to keep Shady Meadows."

Her brother leveled her with a stern look. "You have to keep Shady Meadows, Jewels."

Julie rose, grabbed her mother's hand, and pulled her close. "What about you and Dad? You should get something, too."

Mom smiled. "Dad and I don't need anything. You and your brother will be happy doing what you both love. Elaine and Fred made that possible. *That* was their gift to your father and me."

Tears welled in Julie's eyes again. God had made a way for her to keep Shady Meadows when there seemed to be no way at all. Because, apparently, it had been His plan for her all along. She was filled with awe and gratitude. Like the sun on a brilliant summer day, the Lord illuminated her mind to see the truth. He had placed the desire in her heart for what He wanted to give her.

Now, if He would help her see Derrick as merely a client. Because she couldn't imagine he was the man God planned to give her. She and Derrick didn't make sense. If only her heart would accept what her head already knew. He wasn't a Christian, and he'd always be a cop. Even if Julie did finally understand her dad a little better, she still didn't want the life of a cop's wife.

Derrick was late. Julie glared at the clock. Four forty-five. Fifteen minutes late. Why didn't he call to explain? Didn't he know she'd be worried?

Lord, he's not coming from work, is he? He goes on at eleven. He's safe, right?

Her hands were shaking like saplings in a hard wind. She'd have to share that comparison with Derrick. Not exactly accurate, but definitely not a cliché. He was rubbing off on her. Which wasn't appropriate or professional.

She sank onto the sofa in the reception area, hugged her knees to her chest, and closed her eyes. *Please let him be okay. I ... I can't stop caring about him just because he's not the right one for me. Protect him, Father, please.*

The bell above the door jingled, and Derrick entered with the shepherd. Sadie barked. Derrick shot her a concerned look.

Julie jumped up. She wanted to run into Derrick's arms and weep with relief, but she stiffened instead. Why wasn't God helping her get her feelings for Derrick under control? The man was wreaking havoc on her simple, orderly life.

He closed the distance between them in seconds. With Sadie nudging her knee and Derrick rubbing her shaking hands, Julie couldn't speak. She sucked in a deep breath, yanked her hands free, and snapped, "Why didn't you call me?"

The concern in his eyes changed to surprise and then to satisfaction so fast she almost missed the sequence. The next instant, his composed cop face was firmly in place.

"I didn't call you because the battery in my cell phone died. Sadie chewed up the charger last night, and we had to swing by the store to buy a new one."

"Oh, I thought—"

"You thought something happened to me."

She shook her head. "I thought you forgot your appointment." God would have to forgive her for lying because He certainly didn't want her to tell Derrick the truth and betray the fact that her feelings for him went far beyond those for a client. Or for a friend.

❈

Derrick would let her save face, but she cared more than she wanted him to know. She was fighting her feelings for him. And that was good. That meant he had a chance.

"I'm sorry we're so late. We got caught in a traffic jam, an accident on Genesee Street. Both drivers were okay, and there were no passengers hurt. But the cars were backed up about a mile, what with rush hour traffic and all."

Julie nodded. She reached for the notebook he'd tucked under his arm. "Is this your journal?"

"Yeah, but it may not be exactly what you're expecting."

"I'm sure it's fine. I need to know how things went, how Sadie responded, how you guided her to the correct response. Stuff like that." Julie thumbed through the three pages of his notes. She recorded his arrival time on Sadie's chart. She was stalling, composing herself with the details of her job.

"Do we have enough time to review the lesson on sit-stay that we started on Friday?"

She smiled, the tense lines in her forehead gone. "Sure, but today, we're going to have you leave the room and expect Sadie to hold her stay. Which takes repeated practice because shepherds tend to be Velcro dogs."

"Velcro dogs? What does that mean?"

Julie stroked Sadie's noble head. "It means they want to be with their owners. All of the time."

Derrick laughed. "Aah! That explains why she follows me everywhere."

"Like I said, this will take a lot of practice because, in some respects, we're actually asking her to do something that goes against her nature."

"How long is this going to take?" he asked, releasing a groan. But he was secretly glad because more practice meant more time with Julie.

She ignored his feigned complaint. "For some dogs, several brief sessions daily for a few weeks."

"Oh? In that case, I think Sadie and I will need more than two lessons a week."

Julie shook her head. "You'll be fine with your scheduled lessons."

Her closed-off professional tone would have discouraged him in the past. Now, he chose to trust the Lord. If they were meant for each other, Julie would come around eventually. With God's help, Derrick could be patient when he needed to be. "Slow and steady wins the race." Wasn't that what the tortoise proved? Derrick would have to go slowly with Julie because she was clearly setting a turtle's pace for them.

"Let's get started," he said.

She grabbed a handful of dog kibble from the covered plastic jar on the top shelf of the bookcase and handed him the food without letting her fingers graze his palm. She was putting distance between them, all right.

A quick glance at the dog toys stuffed in baskets on the shelves reminded Derrick of his initial doubts about Julie being the right trainer for Sadie. But God had known all along that Julie knew her job. And that Derrick would fall in love with her.

She touched his arm to gain his full attention.

He studied her beautiful face, his gaze drifting to her mouth. He wanted to forget his plan and kiss her right then and there.

A warning flashed in her eyes as she backed a few feet away. Had she read his thoughts?

"This lesson has three steps. Let's review what we learned on Friday. Step one, command Sadie to sit on your left side. Hold up your right hand, flat and with your fingers together, palm toward the front of her nose, and say, 'Stay.' After a few seconds, reward her with a treat, and say, 'Good girl. You're so smart. Good stay.'"

He followed her instructions, but the minute he exclaimed, "Good girl," Sadie jumped up on his chest and slobbered kisses all over his face.

"Off," Julie commanded.

Sadie kept licking his face, and Derrick couldn't help laughing.

"Stop encouraging her," Julie directed. "Tell her, 'off,' and gently push her until she's standing with all four paws on the floor."

With his hands urging the exuberant dog to the floor, he commanded, "Sadie, off." The shepherd promptly lay down with her head over one paw and shot him a sad-eyed look.

The dog's wounded demeanor tugged at his heart. "What went wrong?"

"Your tone of voice got her all excited. Keep your voice low and calm. She shouldn't move until you say, 'Okay, release.'"

"That seems pretty simple. Why didn't we have this problem last week?"

"Ironically, that's because last week you were more focused on your job. Now, you're enjoying Sadie's company a little too much. You need to remember to pay close attention to her. Watch her front paws. If she moves a paw, gently poke that paw, and say, 'No, don't move.' This way Sadie knows exactly what she did to earn your firm 'no.'"

Derrick nodded. He was trying to pay attention to Julie's detailed instructions, but she looked so cute wearing jeans and a t-shirt that proclaimed, "Your dog doesn't understand the concept of you having a bad day." She wore her long hair tied in a ponytail, and he wanted to pull it free so it could frame her beautiful face. He wanted to pull her into his arms and kiss her until she kissed him back. "What's step two and three?"

Julie frowned. Was she reading his mind again? Or disappointed at his impatience?

"Step two simply involves making Sadie wait longer for her treat. Gradually increase the time you expect her to wait before you praise and reward her. For her to succeed in pleasing you, you must watch carefully for signs she may be about to break the stay. You need to offer the next treat before she moves. That's step two."

He slipped the treats into his pocket and rubbed his strong-willed dog between her ears. "What's step three?"

"In step three, you teach Sadie to hold her stay when *you* move away from her. Remember what we did last week?"

She didn't wait for his reply. "First, I want you to lean away from her. Then, gradually add a half-step, a whole-step, and so on until you can walk away from her without her breaking the stay. She should sit until you give the command, 'Okay, release.' Your goal is to be able to walk several feet away and eventually out of sight into the next room without Sadie following you."

He remembered all of this, but he wanted her to know he was giving her his full attention. "Let me see if I get this. I stay focused on Sadie. If she starts to move, I poke her paw and say, 'No, don't move.' I increase the length of time I expect her to sit-stay before I give her the food, praise her, and say, 'Okay, release.'"

Julie smiled, her eyes shining with approval. How he loved pleasing her! Her smile warmed the whole room. He wanted her smile to be the first thing he saw every morning and the last thing he saw every night. He was beginning to believe things were going according to God's plan. All the events leading up to this moment were fitting together, in surprising ways, all contrary to Derrick's initial plans.

He smiled. If Sadie could learn to hold a stay even when Derrick left the room before Mel and Bob returned from their honeymoon, his sister would be thoroughly impressed. And so would the pretty blonde waiting expectantly for him to continue following her directions.

Under her supervision, they practiced until Derrick could walk several feet away from Sadie. But when he crossed the room to stand beside Julie, his precocious shepherd broke the stay and ran to join them. He wanted to laugh, but he kept his response to a quiet grin. Sadie was falling for her. His dog wanted to be near Julie as much as he did. Derrick resisted the urge to praise his German shepherd for her good taste. They were working on obedience, not affection.

"Try it one more time," Julie said. "You want to end every session with Sadie succeeding and you praising her. We'll need to postpone teaching her to stay when you leave her sight. We can cover that on Friday."

Derrick repeated the sit-stay, but this time he refrained from crossing the room to Julie's side. Following her instructions to the letter was one way he intended to prove to her that she could trust him.

Friday's lesson went better. Derrick could leave the training room for several minutes and return without Sadie breaking her stay until he gave the command to release her. Of course, they'd practiced numerous times at home on Wednesday, Thursday, and Friday before their appointment. Julie complimented him on their excellent progress.

He was pleased with Sadie's progress, too, but not with his own. He'd tried joking and teasing Julie to break down her defenses, but she kept putting up walls, shoring up the boundary she'd imposed from the moment she'd learned he was a cop. Except during their lunch at the park, she'd limited their conversation to the business of training Sadie.

At the end of the session, Derrick closed the front door of Canine Jewels with no indication that Julie would consider a relationship with him once their lessons ended. What exactly would it take to convince her he could be trusted? He'd seen the battle in her sad eyes when she hadn't realized he was watching her. He wanted to comfort her, to tell her they would work everything out together. But her brusque manner had warned him not to get too personal.

Derrick patted Sadie's head. "Let's go home, girl."

As he drove away, he prayed. *Lord, how do I persuade Julie to give us a chance?*

Chapter Seven

Julie had two cancellations on Saturday afternoon. Ordinarily, she'd have been concerned about the negative impact on her income, but when the last client left with his Rottweiler mix at three-thirty, she didn't feel a bit anxious. Not about money anyway.

Derrick was a different story. She wouldn't describe the tight feeling in her chest as anxiety exactly. More like a steady ache that increased with each goodbye.

Sitting in her office inputting notes about the Rottweiler's progress, she took herself to task. "I am not falling in love with him. I got scared when he was late Tuesday night because ... because being a cop is dangerous. And he's a good man. A good man who I—" She slapped her hand over her mouth before the words could escape.

Falling in love with a cop who didn't share her faith couldn't possibly be God's plan for her. Derrick didn't go to church. The Bible commanded her not to be unequally yoked with an unbeliever. Keeping her distance should be simple, but getting her heart on board with her head was next to impossible. Giving up Nick had been easy. From the moment she'd caught him cheating on her, she'd decided they could never share a future.

But Derrick showed up in her dreams, dreams that taunted her with happily-ever-after. And her waking hours weren't any easier.

To distract herself, if only for a short while, she decided to head out to the farm. It was too hot to ride the horses, but she could walk through the house and decide what furniture she wanted to keep and be home in plenty of time to have dinner with Jack and her parents before the fireworks.

Half a mile from the farm, her cell phone rang. She recognized Derrick's number. She pressed the button on her steering wheel to connect the call. "Hi, Derrick." She hoped he couldn't tell how nervous she was. So much for being professional. "I'm driving, so …"

"Julie, I called to tell you I'm sorry about Tuesday night. I wanted to tell you yesterday. I promise you that will never happen again."

She kept her gaze focused on the road and swerved slightly to her left to give Mr. and Mrs. Daniels more walking room, though they ambled off the road onto the gravel shoulder. She lifted her hand to wave at her neighbors.

"Julie, did you hear what I said?"

"Um, yeah. You promise me you'll never let *what* happen again?"

"I'll never let you worry like that again. If I'm going to be late, I *will* find a way to call and explain. I promise."

"Derrick … I … You don't owe me anything. But it is easier when clients call if they can't make their appointment on time."

"I'm not doing it because I'm your client. I'm making you this promise because I don't ever want to see you looking that frightened again. I'm promising you as your friend, as someone who cares about you. A lot."

Her breath lodged in her throat. She swallowed. Hard. What else could she say but thank you? Thank you for understanding what it's like to worry about a cop? Thank you for caring about her?

"Thank you, Derrick. I'll see you Monday at four-thirty."

They exchanged goodbyes, and she disconnected the call. Her excitement at deciding which furniture to keep had completely evaporated. Walking through the farmhouse suddenly seemed like another task on her to-do list. She turned her car around in the Daniels' driveway and headed home.

The minute she mounted the front porch steps, she spotted Jack lounging with his long legs propped on the porch railing. A hardback mystery lay open in his lap.

"Back so soon? I thought you were heading out to the farm."

"I changed my mind."

Jack's brows knit together in concern. "Jewels, what's wrong?"

If only her brother hadn't inherited their parents' observation skills. Sometimes, it was downright annoying, and the only way to conceal anything from Jack was to avoid him altogether. And since he was leaving in a few days, hiding out wasn't an option Julie was willing to consider. She probably wouldn't see him again until Thanksgiving. If he could get away.

It didn't help that accurate discernment was a gene that had completely bypassed her. She shook her head in dismay. Surely, perceptiveness would have been extremely useful in assessing the character of the men in her life. She could pick up dogs' cues, but when it came to men, something misfired in her brain.

"What's wrong?"

"Nothing's wrong. I'm hot, tired, and frustrated."

"There's more than that going on." Jack moved to the porch swing and patted a spot next to him. "You'd rather talk to me than to Mom or Dad, right?"

Julie laughed. "Of course." She sat next to him, leaned close, and planted a quick kiss on his scruffy cheek. "I've missed having you around. You help me figure out what I think instead of telling me what I should think."

"Thanks. So, spill it, Jewels."

Now that she'd agreed to talk to her brother, she didn't know how to begin. "I met him about two weeks ago."

Jack grinned then feather punched her shoulder. "This is about a guy?"

Her face flamed. She reached for Jack's lemonade, took a long swig, and set the empty glass on the table. "Don't sound so shocked."

"Sorry. But you haven't mentioned anyone since Nick."

She nailed her brother with her sternest big sister gaze. "That's exactly the problem. This is Nick all over again. I'm twenty-seven, old enough to know better."

"Know better than what?"

"Than to fall in love with someone who doesn't believe in God, that's what. Now, what exactly do you advise I do about my lousy judgment when it comes to men?"

Jack put up his hands. "Whoa. Slow down. Why don't you start by telling me how you met this guy? What's his name?"

"Derrick. Derrick Walker. He's a cop. And he works with Dad. How could I have let this happen? He doesn't go to church and—"

"We've established you did not meet him at church."

She suppressed a chuckle and slapped her brother's arm. "Stop trying to make me laugh."

"You didn't meet him at the station's picnic because

that isn't until the middle of August." Jack's features lit up with sudden understanding. "He's one of your clients."

She nodded, impressed with her brother's powers of deduction, and disgusted with her total failure to guard her heart. "Yes, he owns a sweet German shepherd."

"And you've been spending a lot of time with them."

She smiled. She couldn't help it. Spending time with Derrick had become one of her favorite occupations. And when she wasn't with him, he was her number one preoccupation. Ever since she'd decided God wanted her to keep Shady Meadows, what to do about her feelings for Derrick had risen to the top of her list of problems needing a speedy resolution. Unfortunately, she didn't have a clue what to do, short of trying to maintain her professional distance, and she wasn't sure whether she was succeeding with that plan. Whenever they were together, Derrick still looked at her as if they were the only two people in the world.

"So, what do you think I should do? Marrying a man who doesn't share my faith isn't an option. And I ... I promised myself I would never marry a cop."

Jack shrugged. "Tell that to your heart."

For the next ten minutes, they discussed her difficult position. Jack offered no advice, but he promised to pray she would have wisdom to discern the truth about Derrick's spiritual condition.

Jack tapped his watch. "Mom will be calling us in for dinner any minute."

As if on cue, their mother shouted from inside the house, "Five minutes until dinner's ready. Come inside and get washed up."

They smiled at their mother's predictability. When Dad was home, dinner was on the table precisely at six o'clock, not a minute earlier or later.

"You're a strong woman, Jewels." Jack took her hand and squeezed it. "If Derrick isn't a Christian, you won't see him anymore after the dog lessons because no matter how much you love each other, not sharing your faith with him will hurt you both in the long run. But if you're wrong, and he is a believer, he may be the man God intended for you. But you'll never find out if you aren't even willing to go on one date."

Julie stopped with her hand on the screen door. "Thanks for the talk, Jack."

"I hope I helped."

"You did. I needed a fresh perspective, one that wasn't clouded by memories of Nick."

Jack nodded and followed her into the house.

Derrick hadn't been to bed after his crazy July 4th shift, which had included eight complaints lodged against neighbors firing off noisy fireworks after two a.m. But he could sleep later. Fighting fatigue, he showered and dressed for church.

Online, he'd found Faith Tabernacle's address. But

second-guessing caused him to doubt the wisdom of going to the church Julie attended. He could check out Leon's church, but then, she wouldn't know he'd gone at all unless he brought it up to her, and that wouldn't work. Derrick needed to show Julie he'd made things right between himself and God. Actions would speak more effectively than words.

Derrick settled Sadie in her crate. The shepherd thumped her tail in displeasure, and he ran his hand along her spine, but she shifted away, refusing his affection. "I'll be back soon, girl," he said in a calm, reassuring tone. "I'm going to church."

He filled his travel mug with his third cup of coffee and headed out, praying the caffeine would keep him from dozing off during the sermon. That certainly wouldn't make a good impression.

It had been a grueling night, with six DWIs, one convenience store hold-up, and a nasty spousal abuse case that had netted him a black eye.

Julie would be upset when she saw his bruised and swollen face. Her compassion might eclipse her shock at seeing him at church. But he suspected it wouldn't play out that way. She'd be upset because he'd been in a dangerous situation, but she would still question his sudden attendance in church, any church, but especially hers.

❀

Julie's eyes were closed for the opening prayer when she sensed someone slip into the pew next to her.

Derrick! It couldn't be.

But it was. No one else smelled that good. The carpet had muffled his steps. He was beside her all right. Here? In her church? Sitting so close. If she moved, her hand or her arm would surely brush against him. She had never been this affected by Nick's presence. She'd never felt so ... so connected to any man.

The minute Pastor Steve said, "Amen," Julie opened her eyes and scowled at Derrick. But he looked so good her anger diminished to mere annoyance. His face in profile was model perfect. He was wearing a crisp white, buttoned-down dress shirt with a navy silk tie and creased gray pants. She'd never seen him in anything but jeans or khakis and a t-shirt. He was so handsome her heart raced with the speed of a greyhound.

He had a lot of nerve coming into her church and sitting next to her as if she were his girl. Clinging to her indignation like a lifeline, she whispered, "What are you doing here?"

"Hopefully, learning how to be a better Christian."

Her stomach flip-flopped. He couldn't be. He'd never said one word about church or believing Christ had died for him. But neither had she. Of course, plaques proclaiming her faith adorned Canine Jewels' walls, and Derrick had seen her reading her Bible that first day at the park. Surely, if he were a believer, too, he would have said something before now.

So why, on this particular Sunday, did he choose to show up at her church? She resisted the urge to clench her hands.

Not again, Lord, please. I can't go through this again.

Julie drew in a deep breath to calm her nerves.

Derrick immediately laid his hand on her bare arm. "Are you all right?" he whispered.

She stared at his hand touching her skin. Gentle strength flowed from his warm palm. He meant to reassure her, and his obvious concern chipped away at her resolve to keep him at a safe distance. She managed to nod in reply then quickly averted her gaze toward the choir members who were assembling at the front of the sanctuary. They started to sing, signaling for the congregation to join them, but Julie didn't trust her voice.

And she definitely couldn't meet Derrick's enquiring gaze. She wasn't ready for him to see into her heart. Not until she was sure they could be more than partners in Sadie's training.

From her other side, Jack elbowed her. "Hey, why aren't you singing?"

She angled a look at her brother. "That's him."

Jack's mouth formed a perfect, silent "O."

The choir sang two or three songs, but by the time they reclaimed their seats, Julie couldn't remember a single word. One memory filled her mind. Derrick's rich tenor singing praises to God. Was he as sincere as he sounded?

When Pastor Steve started his sermon, she managed to refocus her attention on what the Lord might want to say to her. She didn't see how the pastor's current study on Paul's missionary journeys would provide any help for her situation with Derrick. But the Psalms were filled with promises about God helping believers the moment they cried out to Him. And Julie needed help right now. She needed wisdom, guidance, and peace. Right now.

All because Derrick was sitting beside her. And she was happier than she'd been in a long time.

Could she, should she let herself be happy he was here, with her, in God's house? Or should she repair the crumbling wall she'd erected between her and this captivating man?

"Turn to Acts 16," Pastor Steve told the congregation, "and we'll read the entire chapter."

Beside her, Derrick opened a well-worn Bible to the book of Acts then flipped to the correct chapter.

He'd brought his own Bible? Surely, that meant something. On the other hand, it could have belonged to a family member—his mother or his father maybe. Still, he seemed to be following closely as the pastor read. The fact that he'd found the right page without leaning over and asking her for help suggested he was familiar with the Bible.

"The first thing we notice in this passage," Pastor

Steve said as he pointed to various spots on the map displayed on the large screen behind him, "is that the Holy Spirit provided Paul and Silas with clear directions on where to go and where not to go as they traveled from city to city."

It was true. Paul had wanted to go to Asia and Bithynia, but God had made it clear they should go to Macedonia. But Paul had had a vision. Julie was pretty sure the Lord would *not* send her a vision telling her Derrick Walker was a make-believer.

Derrick is not Nick.

She frowned. Was that her thought or God speaking to her heart?

Trust Me, daughter.

She stilled her trembling hands by lacing her fingers together in her lap. Was getting close to Derrick part of God's plan? What if becoming involved with Derrick was simply what *she* wanted? What had Katie said when they'd talked about whether Julie should sell Shady Meadows? Something about having peace if she'd made the right decision. With Derrick sitting beside her, she couldn't describe her current mindset as peaceful.

But throughout the remainder of the sermon, she listened and prayed for guidance and wisdom and for them both to grow closer to God. But mostly she prayed the Lord would protect her from another devastating relationship.

After the closing prayer, when Julie opened her

eyes, she expected Derrick to be nervous, but his features were relaxed. How could he be so calm? Sitting next to her in church as if they were a couple? How could he be so self-assured while she was as jittery as a schoolgirl?

Breathe, Julie. Just be normal.

"I've never seen you here before," she said. That was borderline rude. She wanted to tell him she was glad to see him, but she couldn't risk him taking her admission the wrong way. "Are you looking for a new church?"

"Something like that." He shifted his body and faced her.

She gasped. She hadn't seen more than his right profile until this moment. His left eye was purple and black and swollen nearly shut. "What happened to your eye?"

He shrugged. "It's nothing. An abusive husband didn't want to go to the station. His wife looks a lot worse than I do. Which is why I didn't mind intercepting a left hook meant for her."

Julie fought a wave of nausea. Derrick dealt with violent situations on a regular basis. But he was well-trained. She had to trust him.

And she needed to work harder at trusting the Lord in situations over which she had no control.

"I was never in any real danger. My partner, Leon, was with me, and we'd dealt with this couple before. At least this time, the wife agreed to press charges."

Growing up the daughter of a police officer, Julie

knew some women were too afraid to press charges, afraid their husbands would go through with whatever horrible threats they'd made to coerce and terrorize their wives. "I'm glad she didn't back down. Dad says it's beyond frustrating when a woman won't let the police do their job."

"That's an understatement."

Jack poked her between her shoulder blades, and Julie introduced him to Derrick. Before she could guess his intention, her brother had invited Derrick to go out with their family for Sunday brunch.

She didn't have a chance to get mad at Jack because Derrick's questioning eyes were focused solely on her. He was giving her the space to withdraw the invitation. She smiled to assure him of his welcome. "Please join us."

He responded with a dazzling smile. "I thought you'd never ask."

Warmth flooded through her. Perhaps, God had prompted her brother to extend the invitation she wouldn't have made herself. Jack had never been the matchmaking type, maybe because he was three years younger than she. On the other hand, her little brother, who would soon be taking the bar, probably wanted to check out the man who had captured his sister's heart. Jack had assured her that he trusted her judgment, so his protectiveness didn't rankle the way it had when she'd introduced him to Nick all those years ago. She gave herself a mental shake. Derrick was not Nick, and she wasn't the same girl who'd mistaken charm for character.

Julie was listening to Derrick and Jack discuss their favorite baseball and football teams when her parents joined them. "Mom, this Derrick Walker. Dad, you know Derrick, right? Jack's invited him to brunch."

Surprise flickered in Dad's eyes. Instantly, he composed his features into a blank expression, nodded to Derrick, and addressed Julie. "So, how do you know Officer Walker?"

She flushed with embarrassment but resisted the urge to hide her red cheeks. Her parents knew her rule about not dating clients. And she hadn't dated much at all since college. Naturally, Dad would be curious, Mom more so.

"They're training his German shepherd," Jack said, coming to her rescue.

She shot her brother a grateful look, and before Mom or Dad could ask any more questions, Jack ushered them outside to their cars.

Julie was glad she'd driven her own car. She needed a few minutes to tamp down her nervous excitement. Brunch with her family wasn't a date, but it would give Julie a chance to gauge the sincerity of Derrick's relationship with the Lord. She'd see how he handled her father's probing questions about the sermon. Maybe then she'd be able to tell if he were attending church to get closer to her.

❈

They had barely given the waitress their orders when Dad said, "I haven't seen *you* in church before, Walker. Have you been attending elsewhere?"

Ugh. Julie couldn't deny where she'd gotten her rudeness.

"I haven't gone to church in years."

Mom frowned at the implications.

But Derrick didn't notice. He stirred sugar and cream into his coffee then addressed her father. "I stopped going when I left for boot camp."

"I see. You grew up going to church. What happened to change your mind about God?"

Dad's tone sounded like an interrogation. This wasn't going well at all. Julie nudged her mother under the table, but Mom ignored her not-so-subtle request to change the subject.

Julie shot Derrick a sidelong glance. He didn't appear distressed or uncomfortable. Clearly, he could handle her dad without her help. All right, then. If Dad insisted on grilling Derrick, maybe she'd find out if he'd come to church today only to please her.

While they waited for the server to bring their meals, Julie listened attentively as Derrick explained how he'd blamed God for his parents' deaths and afterward had only attended church with his grandparents out of respect for them.

That part didn't surprise her. Derrick wasn't the rebellious type. He'd sacrificed for his sister ever since their parents' deaths. And probably before that, unless Julie missed her guess.

Why was he sharing this information now when he hadn't mentioned it to her? Was it because, that day at the park, she hadn't given him a chance? Or had something happened since then?

The server arrived with their food, interrupting Derrick's story. After the young woman set their orders in front of each of them, she said, "Let me know if you need anything else."

"We're good," Jack said.

The woman smiled, her eyes resting overly long on Jack's face. When he didn't respond, she headed to her next table.

"She was into you," Julie teased.

Jack raised one eyebrow. "Maybe. But she's too young for me."

Mom scowled at them both, then bowed her head, and Derrick followed her lead.

"Lord," Dad prayed, "please bless this food and the hands that prepared it. May all of us at this table be truly thankful for your provision and protection."

A chorus of soft amens followed. Including Derrick's. Hope leapt in Julie's heart.

Mom buttered her toast then glanced across the table at Derrick. "And when you weren't living with your grandparents—"

"I decided I wouldn't enter any church again until I truly wanted to be there." Derrick cut off a hunk of sirloin steak, dipped it into the runny yolk, and popped it into his mouth. His gaze briefly met Julie's.

She should say something to assure him she understood. Hadn't she blamed God for her aunt's death? She hadn't stopped going to church, but she'd let her fear and anger turn to doubt and mistrust. How difficult it must have been for Derrick to lose both his parents so tragically. She couldn't imagine that kind of grief. She'd lived with the fear of losing her dad, but she'd never been afraid something would happen to her mom.

She slipped her left hand under the table and brushed Derrick's knee. He slanted a broad smile at her, and embarrassed by her bold, supportive gesture, she withdrew her hand and returned her attention to her waffles and fresh strawberries.

"So, what happened to change your mind?" Dad asked.

Unlike the rest of them, he hadn't eaten a bite yet. Not surprising. Her father didn't multi-task.

"When I met your daughter, sir, I started to question whether I was happy running my own life. Focusing on work, and watching over my sister, used to be enough for me."

Dad's grave expression confirmed Julie's fears. He didn't approve of Derrick's interest in his daughter. Dad's protective instincts had shifted into warp drive. But he didn't say a word. His silence made Julie's palms so sweaty she wiped them on her skirt.

"It's not enough anymore," Derrick said at last.

"Is that a fact?" Mom leveled a skeptical look at him.

But Derrick didn't flinch. "Yes, ma'am."

"And what exactly does—"

With her foot, Julie kicked her mother's ankle under the table.

"Meeting Julie made me realize God has good plans for me." Derrick glanced from her mother to Julie. "But I couldn't expect to be in the right place for Him to fulfill those plans until I let Him back into my life."

His eyes searched her soul, as if he could read all the longing and disappointment she'd hidden since Nick had trampled her hopes.

Refusing to cry in front of everyone, Julie pushed her chair back, and stumbled to her feet. "Excuse me. I need to use the ladies' room," she whispered and hurried away before her mother could follow.

Derrick stared after Julie. He ached to intercept her, to take her in his arms and reassure her that he would never hurt her.

Then it hit him. Some man had hurt her deeply, so much that she responded like a skittish barn kitten, ready to run at the first hint of a threat. Or even at the first declaration of interest. He'd have to move slowly to prove he was nothing like that other guy.

"Our daughter's been hurt before," Mrs. Barnes said.

Detective Barnes shot his wife a warning look.

Derrick could imagine what her mother had been about to share, but he wanted to hear Julie's history from her. When the time was right, he would ask her. Better yet, when she felt comfortable with him, she would tell him whatever she thought he needed to know.

Jack met Derrick's eyes then started up a conversation about the family's plans to attend his graduation the following spring. Grateful for the distraction, Derrick concentrated on his steak and eggs and tried not to worry about Julie.

When she returned to their table a few minutes later, he leaned close to whisper, "You seemed upset. Is everything okay?"

She nodded, her features surprisingly composed and relaxed.

Apparently, she'd dealt with whatever had shaken her up. Had she retreated to the restroom to pray? He hoped so. She needed comfort that, even if he were her husband, he couldn't fully give. God alone had to be her ultimate source of peace. Especially if Derrick could persuade her to break her vow never to marry a cop. But first he'd have to get Julie to go out on a real date.

She was quiet as she finished her waffles while the rest of them chatted over more coffee. Jack kept the conversation light, telling funny stories about all the ways he'd teased his sister growing up.

"You still tease me. Every chance you get."

Jack shrugged. "Can you blame me? You're so gullible."

She shook her head and landed a light punch on his arm.

Jack ignored her and asked Derrick if his sister were as easy to tease as Julie was. He dug into his memory for a couple of humorous stories to share.

After Julie finished her meal, Detective Barnes signaled the server to bring the check. He paid the bill and reached for his wife's hand. "Come along, Liz. Let's catch that new romantic comedy you wanted to see."

As soon as they were out of earshot, Jack said, "Say, Derrick, would you like to go horseback riding with me and Jewels this afternoon?"

"Derrick probably has other plans." She leveled him with a look that said don't you dare accept.

"Not really."

"You and Sadie haven't perfected her sit-stay yet, have you?"

Derrick resisted the urge to tease Julie. "Nope, but we're working on it."

"Then, I think—"

"You think I should take a break and go riding with you and your brother out at Shady Meadows?"

Julie's blue eyes widened in surprise.

But her brother grinned. "So, Julie's told you about the place she inherited from our aunt and uncle."

"Actually, I haven't mentioned it." Her eyes filled with questions. She expected an explanation.

There was no way to backpedal. "Ms. Morrison showed me your farm. It's perfect. It's the best place I've seen."

Realization dawned on Julie's beautiful face. "You were the potential buyer."

"You're not mad, are you?"

"Why would I be? You had no idea when you viewed Shady Meadows that I would change my mind about selling."

"If you don't mind my asking," he began, resisting the urge to lay his hand on her arm. She had shivered at his touch earlier, and he didn't want to fluster her in front of her brother. "Why did you put it up for sale in the first place if you didn't want to sell it?"

"She was trying to be fair to me," Jack said. "She didn't know I'd already received my inheritance."

Derrick was about to respond, but Jack's phone rang, and he excused himself to take the call.

"Did the realtor tell you if I did buy Shady Meadows that I didn't want all of your horses?" Derrick leaned close to Julie. Her light floral perfume sent his thoughts in an entirely different direction. *Get a grip, Walker. Now isn't the time to be thinking about running your fingers through those delightful curls.*

"You didn't want all the horses?" she sputtered. "But they've been together forever."

"And no one rides them, not in years, right?"

"I try to ride at least twice a week. And Jack rides when he's home."

"You have your favorites, right?"

"We do not. What exactly are you getting at? That my horses are neglected? I'll have you know my horses are all exercised and groomed every week."

"So, they're not pasture ornaments?"

"Of course not. Uncle Fred used to let the neighborhood kids ride whenever they wanted. We've got amazing trails."

"But you don't let the neighborhood kids ride anymore, do you? Because there's no one out there, if God forbid, anything should happen? Surely, your brother has advised against it."

She shook her head, pressed her lips together. "Jack's not a lawyer yet."

"I wasn't implying that he'd advise you officially."

This conversation had gone in a direction Derrick hadn't intended. He should back off. But he plunged ahead. "The way I see it, three or four horses would be plenty for the average family, unless you're planning on having a lot of kids."

Her face colored a bright pink. She shoved her chair away from the table. "I hadn't thought much about children yet. Being an old-fashioned girl, I figured I'd wait until I had a husband. Not that it's any of your business."

Jack returned before Derrick could reply. It was probably for the best because he had no idea what had possessed him to criticize her care of her horses. Or to bring up children. Or to make her blush with embarrassment. He was out of practice flirting. If he'd ever known how.

"Sorry you two, but I'm going to have to bow out of our plans. Something more pressing has come up," Jack said and winked at Julie.

"In that case," she began.

Derrick wanted to ignore her wary expression, but he'd promised God he wouldn't push her too fast. "I hope you don't mind, Julie, but I think I'd better take a rain check."

The relief sweeping her flushed face assured him he'd made the right choice. She wasn't ready to spend an afternoon alone with him, even if they were on horseback.

Chapter Eight

Fighting loneliness, Julie drove by herself out to Shady Meadows.

Her brother had a date with an old girlfriend.

Her parents were on their own date at the movies, and they'd texted her to say they were planning to drive down to their favorite restaurant on the lake and wouldn't be home until late tonight. Her parents hadn't had a romantic night out in a few months. Julie shouldn't be envious.

But she was.

Because Derrick had gone home or wherever.

Probably because he was a cop, he'd picked up immediately on her signal that she wasn't ready to take their relationship where he clearly wanted it to go.

She parked her car under the towering oak near the

front of Aunt Elaine and Uncle Fred's house.

Her house now.

She should be shouting for joy and thanking God for this amazing gift. But she couldn't stop thinking about Derrick. Hoping a walk through the orchards would help her put everything in perspective, she wandered around back. Seeing the neglected tire swing did nothing to restore her equilibrium. Would she ever push her own child on that swing? What kind of dad would Derrick be? Hands-on? Or exhausted and distracted like her father? Questions she couldn't answer whirled through her mind. Her chest tightened with mounting anxiety.

She needed a quiet talk with the Lord.

A moment later, she entered the barn and greeted all her horses, offering each one a handful of oats and kisses on their velvety muzzles. Derrick's comments about them being neglected still rankled. What did he know about how much she loved her horses? Or how she set up a schedule to ensure that each horse was ridden at least twice a week? There was a lot Derrick Walker didn't know about her.

But there was probably a lot she didn't know about him, too.

She climbed the ladder up into the hayloft. The sweet smell of the season's first hay filled her nose. Determined to unwind, she plopped down onto a stray bale near the loft door and pushed it open with her sandal. A cool breeze and doves cooing in the nearby trees soothed her senses and calmed her agitated mind.

The old barn cat, an orange tabby her brother had named Pumpkin, rubbed the length of her sleek body against Julie's bare legs. With an enigmatic expression, the cat arched her back then lay in the warm sunlight spilling through the loft door.

"So, Pumpkin, Derrick's a Christian after all. And even Dad is okay with one of his fellow officers pursuing his only daughter. Who would have guessed?"

The cat purred, her motor revving up to enjoy a fastidious grooming session followed by a lazy sunbath.

"But that doesn't change the fact that I ... that I what, God? I'm not sure what I feel or think. What exactly am I afraid of?"

She dug into her skirt pocket for a barrette, gathered her thick curls into a condensed mass, then forced the barrette to snap shut over her unruly hair. She closed her eyes to pray and argue and pray some more. Was this what wrestling with God was like?

No, she had to be honest with herself before she could be honest with the Lord. Risking her heart again terrified her. If she could trust Derrick to be faithful to her, if he promised never to leave her, he couldn't guarantee they would grow old together. No man, no matter what his occupation, could guarantee that. But that's what she wanted. A guarantee she could bank her heart on.

If Derrick couldn't give her that, why wouldn't God?

But did she really want to know what the future

held? Wouldn't that knowledge mar the joys of the present?

Exhausted with her feeble attempts to figure it all out, she drew in a deep breath and slowly released it. She envied the old tabby's contentment. Julie couldn't remember when she'd last felt content. Giving up her need for control would be a long process, more than a single act or a single decision.

She dragged over two more bales to form a chair that wasn't exactly comfortable but offered support for her back. Pumpkin, disturbed by the commotion, sulked off. The cat leapt from the loft to the deep pile of straw at the base of the ladder. At twelve, the cat was as limber as she'd been when she'd birthed her first litter in the loft. Impressive.

Relaxing in her make-shift chair, Julie hummed her favorite hymns one after another. As sun lowered in the western sky, the angst that had plagued her for months left, and in its place, an awareness of the amazing magnitude of God's unchanging love brought clarity.

But her muscles started complaining, and her back ached from her awkward position. She checked her watch. It was four-thirty. An hour had passed.

She wasn't ready to admit it out loud, even to herself, but her heart forced her to frame into words the truth God already knew.

If she let herself love Derrick, God could take him away from her. Anytime. The way He'd chosen to take Uncle Fred and Aunt Elaine. And even Toby. Despite all her prayers. Because it was their time. Because God knew more than Julie did.

But she didn't think she could survive losing someone else she loved. Especially Derrick. She already cared for him more than she should.

Everyone she loved was in the Lord's hands. But did she really believe God always does what is best? Until she could trust Him completely, how could she give her love to a man who was prepared every day to sacrifice his life to serve and to protect? A man who could die young, long before she was ready to lose him.

Tears streamed down her face. She pulled folded tissues from her pocket, but it wasn't enough to absorb the flood of grief.

Until she closed her eyes and imagined her Heavenly Father, or maybe His angels, collecting the tears she had refused to release, collecting them into beautiful bottles as the Psalmist declared. What her Father did with those tears, Julie couldn't imagine. But every single tear was surely a shimmering prayer, a pure message she couldn't put into words, a message only her Heavenly Father understood and answered out of His perfect wisdom and love.

For years, she had believed tears were a sign of weakness because others would see how much she cared, and they could hurt her.

She had two choices. Trust God completely. Or live a life crippled by anxieties and fears. She sighed. She was exhausted with trying to control the circumstances in her life, trying to protect herself, trying to pull the yoke alone. Hadn't God promised to work all things together for her good? Including the things that broke her heart. Maybe, especially the things that broke her heart.

She bowed her head and closed her eyes. "Jesus, You've been my savior since I was a little girl. I'm ready to go wherever you lead, to be whoever you want me to be."

An incomprehensible peace settled her heart and mind. She stood, brushed the hay off her clothes, then headed to the ladder. Remembering she'd forgotten to close the hayloft door, she turned back. At that precise moment, a soft gray dove flew inside the loft and lighted on the hay bale where Julie had wrestled with God. Seconds later, the bird flew off, cooing softly. Gazing out the open loft door, Julie allowed herself a moment to drink in the view of the fields, the apple orchards, and the woods beyond.

Feeling freer than ever before, she closed the loft door. Whatever happened between her and Derrick, she could look forward to the future because God's plans, plans He'd designed specifically for her, were good plans. Better than any she could have imagined for herself.

As she made her way, carefully backing down the ladder, she decided to call Derrick the moment she reached her car. Ignoring the horses neighing for more attention, Julie hurried to retrieve her cell phone from where she'd left it on the passenger seat. She found Derrick's name near the top of her contacts list and pressed send.

He answered on the second ring. "Hi, Jewels. I didn't expect to hear from you today."

No one but Jack called her Jewels. But it sounded good when Derrick said it. Like she was precious to him.

"Is everything okay?"

She nodded, then realized he couldn't see her response. "Everything's good. I … I was calling to ask you if …"

"Ask me what?"

"If you'd like to have dinner with me tomorrow after your lesson. You could take Sadie home first, and we'd be able to eat about six or six-thirty. If you still want to go out with me."

"Definitely. You're sure?"

"Yeah. I asked you out, didn't I?"

On Monday night, after they'd completed Derrick and Sadie's initial lesson on come in the training room, Julie went into the restroom to change into a blue and white checked sundress and sandals. She touched up her hair with a drop of smoothing serum, applied a pale pink lip gloss, and slipped on a silver hummingbird necklace inlaid with rainbow mother of pearl. She inserted the matching earrings, then grabbed her white sweater from her office, and considered how well the lesson had gone. It was time to increase the distance between Sadie and Derrick. She preferred to facilitate the next lesson outside, perhaps at the park. That way they could see how far away they could allow Sadie to go and have her still return instantly to Derrick's side at his single use of the come command.

Derrick and Sadie were waiting for her in the parking lot. "I'm ready," Julie said.

Derrick gave Sadie's lead a gentle tug, and they met her halfway. "You look perfect."

"Thanks."

"Makes me wish I had a tie in my glove compartment."

She laughed. "I thought most guys didn't like ties."

"For you, I would gladly wear a tie."

She flushed with pleasure, and he grinned.

"So, I was thinking," Julie said as they walked to Derrick's SUV, the shepherd trotting happily between them, "we don't have another lesson until Friday, but Sadie's ready to try this lesson outside. My last client leaves on Wednesday at six-thirty. Why don't you meet me at the park around seven?"

"We could do that."

He opened the front door, and Sadie promptly jumped up onto the passenger seat. "Get in the backseat, girl. Julie's coming with us, and she gets to ride shotgun from now on."

The shepherd instantly obeyed, and Derrick shot

Julie a dazzling smile that made her pulse race.

He steadied her elbow as she climbed inside, then closed her door, rounded the front of the vehicle, and got into the driver's side. "Sadie's come a long way, hasn't she? You must be pretty proud of us."

Julie returned his smile. "Of course. You two are my best students." What she meant was they were her favorite students, but she wasn't ready to admit that.

He started the car but didn't pull out. "I bet you say that to all of your clients and their dogs."

She chose to ignore the flirtatious gleam in his deep blue eyes. "As a matter of fact, I do. All good teachers recognize the importance of praise. The right amount of praise projects an image for a person, or a dog, to walk into."

He cupped her cheek with his right hand and searched her eyes. "So, we'll become what you imagine?"

His touch warmed her, electrified her, created a hunger to feel his arms around her. She shifted slightly, and he brushed his fingers along her jawline, then gripped the top of the steering wheel again. His satisfied smile declared he was fully aware of the effect he had on her.

With some effort, Julie forced her mind to frame an answer to his question. "Yes, Lord willing, you'll all be good dog owners living in harmony with your dogs. And your dogs will be safe because they will know how to obey your every command."

"That so?"

"Those are my primary goals—harmony, obedience, and safety." She hated to see anyone unprepared for the unexpected, especially if the unexpected was likely to happen. To a dog or to a person. Hadn't that been why she'd refused to date a cop? Because there was no way to prepare for …

"I do remember reading something like that in your contract. The connection between those three elements made sense, though I hadn't ever thought to apply them to my relationship with Sadie."

He pulled out of the parking lot, turned on the radio, and tuned it to a classical station. It was louder than she liked it, and clearly a deterrent to any further talking. Did he like classical music, too? Or was he putting it on to please her? Either way, he wanted to make her happy. But she would be happier with the volume lower, so she turned it down, confident Derrick would be okay with her taking over. "So, what about my idea of a picnic at the park Wednesday night and another lesson after we eat?"

"I've got a better idea." His eyes held hers while they waited for the traffic light to turn from red to green. "Why don't you come to my house for dinner? And after dinner, we'll practice in my fenced backyard. My sister will be home on Friday, and I don't intend to give Sadie a chance to run off."

"You're right. I would have suggested that from the beginning, had I remembered your yard was fenced," Julie said as the light changed.

Derrick refocused on the road. For Julie, the man beside her presented a far more engaging view. His dark hair was long enough that it lay in slight waves against his neck. She imagined her fingers reaching up into his soft hair as he kissed her soundly. Whoa! Hadn't she read about a similar kiss in her book last night, right before she fell asleep? Maybe, but real life would be better.

She smiled so wide she was sure he would guess what she'd been thinking about. To throw him off track, she asked, "So where are you taking me tonight?"

"I thought you might like Fondue Feast. If you've never had their chocolate fondue, you're in for the best dessert experience ever."

The grin splitting his face gave her a glimpse of the boy he must have been before life had left him scarred and guarded. He'd been seventeen when his parents died. Too young to shoulder the responsibility of looking after his younger sister, a responsibility he had accepted willingly, and one he still took seriously, given his statement about Sadie running off.

Ten minutes later he pulled into his driveway. His house, a simple ranch-style, was located on a quiet road in the town of Lancaster. At the far corner of the garage, several Rose of Sharon bushes displayed glorious lavender blossoms. Near the front door, a hanging basket spilled over in a profusion of red, white, and purple petunias. On the opposite post, an American flag waved in the summer breeze.

He parked in the driveway, got out, opened her door, and held her hand as she climbed out of the vehicle. She smiled at his polite gesture. He smiled back then opened Sadie's door. "Come, girl."

As she followed them into the house and waited for Derrick to change, Julie tried to figure exactly how he fit into this peaceful, homey setting. Until she remembered what he had said about his childhood home and about Shady Meadows being the most beautiful place he'd seen. She and Derrick both wanted a sanctuary from their daily stress. Granted his job was far more stressful than hers was, and it always would be.

When they arrived at the restaurant, Derrick requested a table outside. They followed the hostess to a beautiful patio lit with tiny, white lights wrapped around the wrought iron, scrolled railings. More lights were threaded through the potted ivy and bright pink hibiscus plants tastefully displayed in each corner.

It was the most romantic setting she'd ever seen, perhaps a little too romantic for a first date. More than likely, Derrick didn't consider this their first date. They'd had lunch together twice, and now that she was able to be honest with herself, she admitted their planned lunch had been a date.

Fondue Feast was every bit as delicious as the

reviews declared. After an appetizer of yummy breads dipped in tangy cheddar sauce, their dinner included tender chunks of beef and chicken and sliced vegetables, which they cooked themselves on skewers dunked in hot savory broth. The food was scrumptious, but no way was she not going to leave room for dessert.

Moments after clearing away their meal, the server brought fresh coffee, a fondue pot brimming with melted chocolate, a tray of strawberries, banana chunks, and marshmallows, and a second tray of graham crackers, brownies, and pound cake cut into bite-sized squares.

Julie shivered. They had been sitting on the patio for over an hour, so she reached for her coffee first, hoping the hot beverage would warm her up. The night air had chilled her bare arms, bare legs, and bare sandaled feet. Summer evenings in mid-July were usually much warmer.

"You're cold," he said, dunking a speared strawberry into the warm chocolate. He popped it into his mouth. "Didn't I see you with a sweater in the car?"

Before she could protest, he rushed to get it for her. Within minutes, he returned to their table and stood behind her chair holding the bulky sweater while she slipped her cold arms into its cozy warmth. But it was more than the sweater that warmed her. It was his unexpected thoughtfulness. "Thank you for getting my sweater. I feel warmer already."

"No problem, Jewels. It is okay if I call you Jewels, isn't it?"

"Jack's the only one who calls me Jewels, but if you like it ..."

Derrick smiled.

It was a small concession, but giving him permission to use her nickname increased the intimacy between them exponentially. Surprisingly, she didn't mind. She dipped a banana slice in the gooey chocolate and held it across the table to offer it to him.

"I don't like bananas." He wrinkled his nose, making her wonder again what he'd been like as a young child.

"Try it. If you don't like it, I promise to look the other way so you can spit it out into your napkin."

He laughed, shook his head, opened his mouth, and bit it off her skewer. "Not bad. But not exactly good either."

It was her turn to laugh.

"I think we're both learning to try new things, aren't we?" he said.

His gaze on her face made her cheeks heat with a blush. She was learning to trust God to direct her in her relationship with Derrick. Could he possibly know how hard it was for her to relinquish control? And if he knew that much, did he also guess how much she wanted to yield her heart to him?

After their date, Derrick was wired for the third shift. Monday nights were usually quiet after the craziness of the weekend, which was good because Leon looked exhausted. His mouth was drawn into a thin, grim line. His three girls had been battling the twenty-four-hour stomach flu that day, and Tamika hadn't been able to take off work.

"Some project she couldn't postpone or delegate," Leon grumbled. "So, I had to be on clean-up duty all day. Good thing God gave me a cast-iron stomach."

Derrick's stomach flopped. "Too many details, Martin."

"At least you didn't have to be there."

Derrick finally got the message. Although it wasn't his turn, he said, "Pull over, and I'll drive."

At three-ten a.m., after a typically quiet Monday night, Tuesday morning, whatever he wanted to call it, Derrick clocked a white Buick going fifty in a thirty-five-mile speed zone.

He glanced at Leon.

"Yeah. I know what you're thinking. This is odd for a Monday."

"And the driver hasn't swerved once."

This was an emergency, more than likely a medical emergency.

Leon switched on the flashing lights. The driver instantly pulled over, parking the Buick behind a rusted Chevy station wagon. Derrick hadn't seen one that old in years. The houses on both sides of the street were dark. Not a soul in the neighborhood stirred. Good thing he hadn't used the siren.

The driver, a young man who couldn't be much more than twenty, exited the Buick and rushed toward the squad car. Derrick flung the door open and met the man halfway.

"Thank God. Come on."

Raising his eyebrows, Derrick planted his feet and waited for the distraught man to catch his breath and explain.

"My wife's having a baby. She says—"

"My partner and I will give you a police escort to the hospital." Derrick silently thanked the Lord that he and Leon had arrived at precisely the right time. They'd escorted couples to the hospital before. At least a half dozen times in the last five years, if his memory could be trusted. "Get back in your car, wait for us to start down the street, then pull out right behind us. We'll run the lights and the siren. Ignore the stop signs and traffic lights and keep right on going behind us. We'll have you there in ten minutes."

The young man shook his head. "No. She can't wait. She can feel the head." The distraught father grabbed Derrick's hands, pleading, "*You* have to deliver my baby."

A scream of pain pierced the silent night. Several lights flicked on in nearby windows. The frightened man raced to his wife. Derrick waved Leon out of the squad car. In his hand, Leon carried the emergency medical kit.

"You heard?"

"Yeah. Already made the 911 call."

Derrick faced his partner. "This one is all you, man."

Leon shook his head, clapped his hand over his mouth, bent behind the squad car, and started retching. A moment later, he straightened and wiped his mouth on a wad of tissues. "I can't do it. Must've got what the girls have." And he doubled over and puked again.

Derrick had never delivered a baby before. He'd watched Leon deliver a set of twins last summer, but to guide a newborn into the world himself ... He couldn't do it.

The woman screamed again.

"Officer, I can see the head," the man shouted, his voice clearly rousing the neighborhood as more lights glowed in windows along both sides of the street. "Oh, sweet Jesus, help us."

Leaning against the trunk of the squad car and holding his stomach, Leon groaned. "You can do this, Derrick. God will help you. Go do your job. Now."

With the emergency kit tucked under his arm, Derrick strode toward the couple, praying for God's hands to be over his hands, for the Lord to guide him and to help him bring this baby safely into the world.

Derrick touched the young husband's shoulder, eased him aside, then knelt on the street before the woman's spread knees. The baby was crowning. He didn't have much time. A few minutes at most. He opened the kit, checked for the surgical clamps and the scissors. Quickly, he pulled on gloves, opened a sterile pack, unfolded a large sterile pad, gently lifted the woman, and positioned the pad beneath her. He unwrapped the sterile drape and covered the woman from her chest to over her knees.

"I've … got … to push!"

"Not yet." Derrick positioned his hands, ready to ease this new person into the world. "Okay, push."

With her husband at the other end of the backseat supporting her shoulders, the young mother gave two quick pushes, groaning and screaming.

The head emerged.

God, no.

The cord was wrapped twice around the baby's neck. The tiny face, pale blue. "Stop. Don't push."

The woman shuddered, leaned against her husband, and wept. "I need to push!"

"Do *not* push," Derrick commanded. He caught the husband's frightened gaze, and mouthed, "Whatever you do, don't let her push."

Derrick touched the cord. Tight, too tight to unwind now. He'd have to let her push again. At the precise instant the baby's shoulders slipped out, he'd need to get the cord off its neck.

"I have to push now!"

"Okay, push."

Derrick's left hand cradled the baby's head. His right hand guided the first shoulder, then the other. He yanked a length of cord to create slack. His hands moved swiftly. Gently unwinding one loop, then the second from the baby's neck.

The face. Not pink. "Push. Once more."

"I can't."

Her husband urged, "Just one more, honey. You can do it."

She howled, pushing.

The wet, slippery baby girl slid into Derrick's waiting hands. He placed her on her mother's stomach on the sterile drape. She let out her first tiny cry. Derrick blinked back tears of relief and incredible joy. He attached two clamps to the cord, spaced about three inches apart, and made a clean cut between the clamps. Too late, he realized he should have asked the young father if he wanted to cut his daughter's umbilical cord.

"Our baby's here," the woman cried, looking first at the child and then at her husband.

"Is our baby all right?" she asked.

"Your baby is perfect. Ten fingers. Ten toes," Derrick pronounced. "She's beautiful."

Her pink cheeks proclaimed the miracle.

He had never seen any child so beautiful. Relief rushed through him. *Oh, Father, thank You for letting me experience this miracle of life. Thank You for showing me what to do.*

The husband bent to kiss his wife's cheek. "I want to hold my baby," she said, reaching her hands out for her precious child.

Derrick quickly dried the little one off with a sterile towel then wrapped her in a second towel. Gently, he lifted the baby girl into her mother's waiting arms. Mother, father, and baby created an unbroken circle of love.

Derrick brushed away his own tears. *Lord, thank You for bringing us here at the exact time, when we were needed. Thank You for using my hands to save this baby's life.*

A time to be born …

And a time to die …

He understood at last.

Chapter Nine

Tuesday morning, Julie and her mother were maneuvering around each other in kitchen as they prepared to leave for work. Food for breakfast, lunch, and afternoon snacks. That was something she and her mother shared, a high metabolism that required frequent meals to keep them moving cheerfully through their days. They were standing side by side at the counter packing their insulated lunch bags when Julie leaned over and planted a kiss on Mom's cheek.

"What was that for?"

"Because I love you. And I don't tell you enough."

Mom pulled Julie into a one-arm embrace. "Love you, too. And I don't tell you often enough either."

Julie brushed away tears forming at the corners of her eyes. Since she'd prayed in the hayloft, her emotions were uncorked and close to the surface. She wasn't used to feeling so vulnerable and transparent. Thank goodness the rare moment of intense connection between her and Mom passed quickly.

Mom filled her travel mug with coffee then poured a mug to drink right away. She filled a second mug and handed it to Julie. "I must admit I was a little surprised on Sunday."

Julie nearly dropped the coffee creamer. This was going to be some morning.

"Your father's mentioned Derrick to me a few times. 'Derrick Walker is one of the best men in our precinct. No one knows the streets like he does.' That's what your father said."

Julie's stomach clenched. If Derrick were that good, he'd never consider leaving the force. He would always be a police officer.

But she had already known that.

Lord, I trust You to keep him safe. You love him more than I do.

She stifled a gasp and nearly dropped her coffee mug. She did love Derrick, loved him enough to change for him.

Mom patted Julie's arm. "I know."

Her mother understood. She'd been in Julie's position herself once, unsure how she could handle the stress of a relationship with a cop.

Mom pulled out a chair and motioned for Julie to join her at the kitchen table. "Honey, are you sure you know what you're doing? Getting involved with Derrick?"

Soothed by the love and concern evident in her mother's voice, Julie no longer wanted to hide her fears or be ruled by them. "I've prayed so hard about what to do."

"Prayer is always a good place to start." Mom took a bite of buttered toast. "Most of the bad choices I've made happened when I left prayer out of my decision-making process."

Julie agreed. She'd made that mistake many times.

She wasn't hungry now, but she forced herself to eat a few bites of oatmeal, then put the spoon down, and pushed the nearly full bowl aside. "I always said I could never be a cop's wife. How do you do it, Mom? Sometimes, I get so afraid for Derrick I can barely breathe, let alone think rationally."

"I pray a lot, for protection and wisdom for your father," Mom explained. "For myself, I constantly ask the Lord to help me remember He is in control, not me. And He loves your father more than I ever could."

Moments before, Julie had prayed for Derrick in almost the same words. Like her mother, wanting to be in control was half of Julie's problem. She could learn a lot following her Mom's example. If she could let go and let the Lord grow her trust in Him, and stop trying to work herself into that place, faith would defeat her fears and conquer her wrong thinking. She needed more faith because God expected her to yield up everything that was keeping her from being the woman He intended her to be.

And she was starting to hope part of being that woman would be being Derrick's wife.

"I have a sense about Derrick Walker." Mom sipped her coffee, her expression suggesting she was carefully considering her next words. "He's a good man, Julie. And anybody with eyes can see he loves you."

Feeling more exhausted than usual—probably due to coming down from the adrenaline rush of delivering a baby for the first time, Derrick called the department to inform them he would be taking a personal day tonight. That way if his cleaning lady couldn't come by on such short notice, he could sleep as long as his body needed and still have time to cook his spaghetti sauce a day ahead and make his house presentable for Julie. Sure enough, when he sent Sally a brief text, she replied that she already had two jobs lined up, though it was barely eight o'clock. She couldn't possibly squeeze him in today and would not be coming until her regular day the following Monday. A thorough cleaning every other week was usually sufficient, but he wanted to make a good impression. The last thing he wanted was for Julie to think he was a slob. That meant he would have to clean and cook, but both would have to wait. Right now, his priority was taking care of himself and Sadie.

After a shower and a quick breakfast, he took his dog out back to practice loose leash walking. As Julie had warned him, Derrick did more waiting than walking. They would manage two or three steps, and Sadie would race to the end of her lead, trying to catch a foolhardy squirrel or a taunting robin. At first, he had trouble resisting his natural urge to pull the shepherd back to his side. But after about three or four false moves on his part, he remembered Julie's admonition that he stop immediately every time Sadie tugged on the lead and wait for *her* to return to him. But that took a while. His sweet dog amused herself by alternately sniffing and pawing at the ground and scanning the yard for intruders. The sparkle in her dark eyes communicated her clear message. This outing was for her entertainment. Each time, after two or three minutes, Sadie would turn to him and cock her head as if to say, I'm ready to walk again, what about you?

Derrick had to work to keep from laughing. She was such a smart dog.

By the end of the session, they had succeeded in circling the acre lot only four times. The sun was fairly high in the eastern sky. He checked his watch. Ten o'clock. Ninety minutes of walking the dog. He patted her head. "Come on, girl. Let's go inside. You've got to be as thirsty as I am. And I need some sleep."

Loose-leash walking hadn't been nearly as peaceful an experience as he imagined walking a dog should be. Fact was he was bone tired. After they both rehydrated,

Sadie followed Derrick directly to his bedroom, where she took up her post in his doorway, settling down on the thick rug he'd trained her to sleep on. He patted her twice, "Good girl. Time for a nice long nap, okay?"

She rested her head on her paws, and he climbed gratefully into bed, hoping to clear his mind quickly. Working the eleven-to-seven shift, he was usually too keyed up to sleep when he first got home. Sometimes, he would work out, lifting weights and bench-pressing to the classical station's morning wake-up program. Then he'd shower, and by nine-thirty, he'd usually be unwound enough to drift off for the next six hours or so.

But some mornings, he would lie in bed staring at the light diffusing through the shades and illuminating his bedroom walls, and he would wonder what exactly he was doing with his life. He patrolled Buffalo's west side, arresting prostitutes, addicts, and dealers. On a good night, he did his job well, and no one got hurt on his watch. On a bad night, he was forced to use his gun to save somebody's life. On the worst nights, he was too late, too late for some crazy, strung out addict willing to do anything for his or her next fix. Or too late for some innocent bystander who didn't know how insane the world on the streets could be.

Nights like last night were few. Before he'd recommitted his life to the Lord, Derrick would have said they were too few. But such life-giving and life-affirming experiences were not what he expected, were not why he'd signed up to serve and protect. He was born to be a cop.

After six years on the force, he was starting to feel burned out, but he still had the edge and the instincts that had earned him two commendations. He'd been responsible for putting enough drug dealers in prison that he was rarely without his gun. And if he wasn't armed, he knew at least a half dozen ways to kill a man with his bare hands, if he had to. Thankfully, it had never come to that. He relied on his skills at de-escalation to diffuse potentially violent situations. He still believed he had a job to do that few could do as well as he could.

So, he kept on, though some images haunting his dreams were hard to forget, even in the fresh, cleansing light of day.

But today was different. The moment his head hit the pillow, he dreamed of Julie. Laughing, smiling, running in the park, playing ball with him and Sadie. When he finally awoke about four in the afternoon, he sat straight up, Julie's name on his lips. He ached to wake up with her in his arms. Which couldn't happen often because she worked days, and he worked nights. Maybe, he could do something about that if ...

Courting her wouldn't have to take a long time, would it? Derrick wanted to make Julie his wife before the year ended.

❅

Tuesday passed uneventfully for Julie, except for Jack's leaving. They'd eaten lunch in the park together, said their goodbyes, and she was back at Canine Jewels for her two o'clock appointment.

Sitting at her desk reviewing the day's schedule, she already missed her brother. If only he would decide to practice in New York State, somewhere within driving distance. Julie dismissed that thought immediately. Her brother had other plans, and she respected and supported his decisions, as he did hers.

Later that afternoon, the usual chaos ensued during the first session of a new puppy class. Two children in this group were younger than she liked to work with, five and eight. She gave herself a mental pat on the back for limiting the class to five: five children, five puppies, and five parents. But by the time the class ended, she'd decided to revise her class sizes. Going forward, for kids under ten, she would limit the group to three kids, three puppies, and three parents. If she didn't make this change, she'd be gray by the time she turned thirty.

Thankfully, the other two classes and the single private lesson that day went smoothly. Julie finished entering her notes into the computer and locked up in plenty of time to arrive punctually at the bi-monthly ladies evening Bible study at the Candy Apple Café.

Tonight, they were beginning a study on the Proverbs 31 woman. Before she'd met Derrick, she probably would have concocted some excuse to miss this six-week study, mostly because she and her friend, Stacey, were the only single women left in the group. Privately, they'd discussed skipping this study and possibly doing something together that focused on singles, but Stacey had reasoned that they both wanted to be married eventually, so in the end, they nixed the idea of doing a different study on their own.

Julie spotted her friends seated at their usual table in the back. Katie, Vanessa, Taylor, Lexie, and Chloe were studying their menus. Where was Stacey? She was never late. For anything.

The ladies greeted Julie in unison, and she slipped into one of the two remaining seats. A moment later, Julie's phone pinged with a text notification. She fished in her canvas bag until her hand closed around her cell. The text from Stacey simply said, "On my way."

When the server arrived to take their orders, Julie ordered a grilled chicken sandwich for herself and a cheeseburger for Stacey, both with fries, and two glasses of sweetened iced tea with lemon.

Once the server left to put their orders in, Lexie shared her news. She was pregnant already. She and Chuck hadn't planned on having a baby so soon, but she'd conceived sometime during her honeymoon week.

The ladies were fully engaged in discussing plans for a baby shower when Stacey rushed into the restaurant at six-fifteen. She draped her sweater over the chair next to Julie then snagged a menu that effectively hid her face from view. But Julie had seen what her friend tried to hide. Stacey's dark eyelashes were spiked with moisture, and it wasn't raining.

Julie leaned close. "I already ordered for you. Cheeseburger and French fries like always. What's wrong? You've been crying."

"Todd and I broke up. He said he doesn't think we want the same things." Stacey swallowed hard, reached for the iced tea at her place setting, and took a long drink. "He doesn't want a family."

"What? No kids. Not even one?"

"He doesn't even want a dog, let alone kids. He wants to be free to travel. Or to pick up and move across the country if he gets the urge."

Julie clasped Stacey's arm. "That's terrible. I'm so sorry. I know you thought he might be the one."

Stacey shook her head. A single tear rolled down her cheek. "I didn't know him at all."

"This isn't your fault. You don't wait until you've been dating for six months to share information that important. Who knows what else Todd may have hidden from you?"

"You're right." Stacey pushed her menu to the edge of the table. "Listen, Julie, I don't want to talk about this with the others. Not tonight. Okay?"

"Okay."

"So, Stacey, you finally got here." Lexie beamed. "Did you hear my news?"

"I did. You can count on me for flowers for your shower."

"You're the best. Thanks."

By the time the food arrived, each woman had assigned herself a task to ensure that Lexie's baby shower would be perfect. After they finished their meals, Katie read the chapter aloud, and each person in turn offered insights and asked questions.

As the women headed to their cars, Stacey promised to call Julie soon so they could meet for lunch.

During her drive home, Julie pondered two verses that spoke to her: "The heart of her husband doth safely trust in her …. She will do him good and not evil all the days of her life." That was exactly the kind of wife she wanted to be. She didn't want to make it harder for Derrick to do his job by putting him in a position where he had to be worried about her worrying about him. If God meant her for Derrick, she would have to give her worries and fears over to God. As many times as necessary, whenever anxiety and fear threatened to steal her peace.

By six forty-five on Wednesday night, Julie was parking under the shade of a red maple in Derrick's driveway. She shut off the engine, grabbed her canvas bag from the passenger seat, and exited her car wearing a new-found confidence in both herself and the Lord. Her future, including her relationship with Derrick, was in safe hands.

The charming man who'd captured her heart met her on the neatly swept porch. "I heard your car."

He meant her muffler. She needed to replace it. Maybe he could recommend someone. Or, maybe, he knew how to fix it himself. Wouldn't that be handy? "Hi, Derrick."

"Hi, Jewels." He held the screen door open for her, and she strolled past him into his house.

Awareness shot between them, and her pulse quickened at a whiff of his aftershave. *Go slow, girl. No need to let him see how his nearness affects you. At least not yet.*

But his warm expression indicated he was fully aware and felt the same way about her. "Dinner will be ready in about fifteen minutes. I didn't want to start the spaghetti until you got here."

He sounded nervous.

Which only made him more attractive because he was allowing her to see that, like her, he felt vulnerable in this new phase of their relationship. He wasn't the hard-nosed cop she'd first pegged him as. To think her prejudices might have kept her from getting to know the man behind the badge.

"You look beautiful." His gaze traveled from her head to her feet.

Wearing her new Julie's Canine Jewels t-shirt in a soft rose with black jeans and sneakers made her feel underdressed for a date, but Derrick didn't mind. The appreciation in his eyes reduced her disappointment over not being able to wear the new white sundress with the tiny lavender rose print, which she'd bought that morning, together with her favorite strappy sandals that added two inches to her height. If they hadn't planned to train Sadie after dinner, Julie would have gladly worn her new dress to remind him again that she was more than a dog trainer.

But Derrick was wearing jeans, too, and a short-sleeved navy polo shirt that accented his tanned arms and strong shoulders. He had trimmed his dark hair shorter than she usually liked, but on him it was perfect. Too handsome really. Especially with his shadow beard.

Her breath caught in her throat as she imagined being encircled by his muscular arms. She remembered her first impression—that he was strong enough to carry her as easily as he carried Sadie.

"You're blushing."

Her hands flew to her cheeks then fumbled with the straps of her bag.

He stepped closer, so close she could smell cinnamon on his breath. Amusement danced in his eyes. "You do know you were staring?"

She sputtered an apology. "You look pretty good yourself."

"I'm glad you approve."

She did approve, very much. There ought to be a law against a man being able to fluster a woman as much as Derrick was doing now. But what fun would there be in that?

To distract herself from her escalating attraction to him, Julie directed her attention to the simply furnished living room, which she'd been too nervous to take in on Monday. They'd only been at his house less ten minutes, long enough to put Sadie in her crate. Derrick had quickly changed into navy pants and a blue button-down shirt, complete with a silver silk tie. One glimpse and she'd known the best use for a tie—pulling him close for a kiss. She'd had to avert her face to hide the heat that flooded her face and neck. He'd only smiled and said, "Glad you like the tie."

Blushing again at the memory, she pivoted around the room to examine every detail. Derrick's presence was everywhere. A shelf with commendation medals, including his Purple Heart, and photographs of him with a young brunette hung on the wall above a rich brown leather sofa made inviting with several oversized suede pillows. A matching loveseat and a recliner formed a semicircle facing a working fireplace. More family photos were displayed on the mantel and end tables. A large book of impressionist paintings lay on the coffee table next to a James Patterson mystery and a set of inlaid wood coasters.

From behind her, Derrick slipped his arm around her waist and rested his hand lightly on her right hipbone. He directed her to a photo of the brunette sharing a kiss with a handsome blond guy. "That's my sister, Mel, with her new husband, Bob. He's the one that's allergic to Sadie. I didn't know at the time, but that's one of the best things that ever happened to me."

Julie smiled. Derrick had changed so much since their first meeting when he'd been decidedly put out with his dog. She started to tell him how pleased she was, but he guided her toward the fireplace and more photos.

"This old black and white photograph, those are my grandparents, the ones Mel and I used to live with. And that," he said, directing Julie to the largest portrait above the oak mantel, "is me and Mel with our parents. It was taken a month before they were killed."

Julie shifted slightly so she could see Derrick's face. The sorrow in his eyes wrenched her heart. What could she say? A sudden urge to kiss him drew out the silence as his gaze locked with hers.

Finally, she said, "I'm sorry, Derrick. You must miss them so much."

"I do. They were the best." He mustered up a smile. "But we'll talk about them some other time. Why don't you sit down and relax while I finish dinner?"

Respecting his need for space, she nodded. He disappeared into the kitchen, and she perched on the edge of the loveseat. What would it be like to be sitting here with him on a chilly fall night in front of a blazing fire? Her face warmed with a blush that flooded her body with heat. What was wrong with her? She had to get her mind off kissing him.

Helping him with dinner would be a distraction.

Hopefully.

Following the sound of his whistling, Julie entered the kitchen-dining area, a sunny room that ran the length of the back of the ranch-style house. Cream-colored walls adorned with several Monet prints created a soothing, restful atmosphere. Two sliding glass doors at the dining room end provided a perfect view of the spacious backyard, lined with various trees and flowering shrubs.

Derrick stopped whistling and looked up from the tomatoes he was quartering. He smiled, and his attentive expression drew her like a hummingbird to sweet nectar. Why hadn't he kissed her yet? He wanted to kiss her. That much she knew for sure. Maybe he was waiting for a signal from her. Surely, the frequent flame in her cheeks gave a clear indication of her willingness.

"Your home is beautiful."

"Thanks." He scraped the tomatoes off the cutting board and into the salad bowl then started slicing a cucumber. "But it doesn't compare to Shady Meadows."

"I'm glad you like the farm. I've decided to move in, hopefully by the end of this month."

"You've made the right decision. I'm happy for you, Jewels." He added sliced mushrooms and grated a sprinkling of fresh parmesan over the salad. To her astonishment, he proceeded to mix herbs, olive oil, and vinegar for a homemade dressing.

"It took me a long time to decide—to be sure what I wanted was what God wanted for me."

"I can see you have peace about your choice." Derrick turned from his task to focus on her. "That's usually a good indication you're on the right track." His blue eyes sparkled with approval.

And his approval meant a lot.

"Katie said the same thing when I was agonizing over what to do. She said she could see I didn't have peace about selling."

"Smart woman. She's the pastor's wife, right?"

"Yes, and a good friend. I babysit for them at least once a month. Katie leads a ladies Bible study I've been attending since I moved back home after finishing college. She started it for singles, but now, everyone's married but me and my friend, Stacey."

Why had she brought up that detail? Derrick had only asked about Katie out of courtesy.

He dumped spaghetti into the boiling water, added a few drops of olive oil, and stirred until the pasta swirled freely. "So, you do like kids. That's good. I wasn't sure after our discussion at brunch."

If only she weren't so fair. Again, her face heated to a crimson flush. Her neck was warm, too. Thank goodness he was concentrating on dinner preparations. Maybe, she should apologize for overreacting when he'd brought up the subject of how many kids she planned to have. "Derrick, about what I said at the restaurant ..."

He filled two glasses with lemonade and handed one to her. "I was out of line criticizing you about the horses. I know you would never neglect them."

"Thank you. But you're right. I would like to spend more time with my horses, and once I'm settled out there, I'll be able to ride more often."

He drained half of his lemonade. "Maybe, we could ride together sometime."

"I'd like that."

Derrick placed the carafe of dressing and the salad bowl on the table. Then, he lit blue candles in silver candlesticks. Two place settings of white china with scalloped edges, cut glass water tumblers, fine silverware, and pale blue cloth napkins completed the picture of a romantic dinner for two. She could have no doubt of his intentions to woo her.

Apparently unaware of her nervous response to his elaborate preparations, he returned to the stove and tasted the spaghetti sauce. He put the spoon in a second time and held it out to her. "I think it needs something."

He leaned close and placed the spoon in her mouth. Surprised, she savored the sauce a moment. "Maybe a bit more salt."

He added a dash.

Who knew cooking could be so romantic? Her parents rarely cooked together. Sometimes, Dad helped with the cleanup, but washing dishes together didn't rate high on her list of romantic activities. So much for distraction. No matter what they were doing, being near Derrick was more distracting than being with Nick had ever been. Maybe she hadn't given that scoundrel her heart after all.

Now that was a liberating thought. Realizing she hadn't been truly tied to Nick left her free to love Derrick without feeling as if she couldn't trust her own judgment, didn't it?

Julie suddenly noticed that other than the soft classical music streaming from the Alexa, the house was quiet. "Where's Sadie?"

"Out back. Why don't you call her inside?"

Julie approached the sliding glass doors. The German shepherd was about fifteen yards from the back deck. Another twenty yards beyond her a squirrel munched on something, probably a nut. Sadie was poised to run. Julie was certain the squirrel could scamper safely up the maple tree beyond the dog's reach. But she didn't want to take a chance. In seconds, she stepped outside. "Sadie, come!"

The dog bounded across the yard toward the deck. Glad for her sneakers, Julie braced herself for the inevitable collision. But Sadie slowed her pace, climbed up the four steps, and braked to a halt on the deck inches from Julie's feet. The joyful light dancing in the dog's eyes was a marked contrast to the fear Julie had seen less than three weeks ago.

"Good girl, Sadie." Julie patted the dog, who sauntered past her into the house. Amused and relieved, Julie followed.

"What was that all about?" Derrick asked.

"I thought Sadie was going to kill a squirrel, but she came right away when I called. You've made so much progress with her."

"Thanks. We couldn't have done it without your help. And to think I almost walked out of Canine Jewels when I saw your quirky setup."

She smiled. She'd never imagined he would be so teachable. He'd followed all her instructions faithfully. And she had believed all cops thought they knew everything. Apparently, she'd made a lot of wrong assumptions. She'd been unfair, and she'd misjudged him.

"I'm glad you decided to give me a chance." Julie stood beside Derrick as he forked a strand of spaghetti from the boiling water. "Like I told you that first day, as long as you pay attention to Sadie, be in the moment with her, she will know you love her, and she'll do anything to please you."

He broke the spaghetti in half, put one piece in his mouth, and handed her the other. "I think it's done."

He grabbed two potholders from the hooks above the stove, carried the pot to the sink, and poured the spaghetti into a colander. "Dinner should be on the table in ten minutes." He tested the sauce again and added a light sprinkle of oregano.

Without being asked, Sadie wandered into her crate, circled twice, then settled herself on her soft blanket.

Derrick grinned and followed her. He knelt before the crate, face-to-face with the dog. Petting her head, he said, "Good girl. You can come out after dinner."

"Looks like you two are getting along much better."

"Yep. I'm beginning to understand why the guys in K-9 say once you've been loved by a German shepherd, no other dog will do."

Would this man never cease to surprise her? Her concern that he would be unable to open his heart to Sadie had been completely unfounded. "I have heard shepherd owners say that. Of course, a yellow lab can be a sweet companion, too."

He gave her a curious, inscrutable expression and then stirred more parmesan into the simmering sauce.

"What are you thinking?" she asked.

"I already had you pegged as a lab person, that's all."

She hadn't had a dog since Toby, a decision her parents had initially made for the family.

But Julie could have her own dog soon when she moved out to Shady Meadows. By summer's end, she planned to be training her own puppy. And her first choice would be a yellow lab, one who would scamper into her life and enchant her days the way Toby had.

"So, what kind of dog do you have?" Derrick asked.

"We don't have a dog. My brother is allergic to dander."

"Really? I thought that was a rare thing."

"It is. About fifteen percent of people are allergic to dander. Unless you have asthma. Then, the percentage doubles," she explained, glad to focus on facts. After all these years, losing Toby shouldn't still hurt, but she blamed herself. If only she'd shut the puppy in the kitchen. But she didn't get a do-over.

The delicious aroma filling the kitchen stirred her hunger and offered a distraction from lingering sadness over something she couldn't change. "How can I help with dinner?"

"Finish the garlic bread while I pour us more lemonade and put the food on the table."

She chose a spot in the kitchen far away from Derrick so she wouldn't be flustered by his signature aftershave. She found a sharp knife and the cutting board and began slicing the freshly baked Italian bread. He pointed to a small skillet of minced garlic sautéing in butter. This man could really cook. Her dad could scramble eggs or microwave oatmeal. That was about it. Julie liked the idea of being married to a man who would share the cooking. Especially since her own cooking skills were average at best.

Slow down, girl. You just started officially dating the man this week.

She returned to her assigned task and slathered melted butter and sautéed garlic over thick slices of bread. She checked the oven settings. He already had the oven set on broil. She slid the tray of bread onto the top rack.

"Have you ever cooked dinner for anyone else?" Horrified by the question, she wanted to yank the words back. Had she actually asked him about other women in his life? She'd never been the jealous type, but the thought of Derrick with anyone else hurt.

He set the pitcher of lemonade on the table then turned to her. He was so close every nerve in her body responded to his nearness. How could she love this man so much, so soon? They hadn't known each other for three weeks. She stared at her sneakered feet, hoping to conceal feelings she feared he might not share.

With one finger, he lifted her chin. Could he see the confusing emotions wreaking havoc on her normally composed features?

His expressive eyes declared his interest. "Only for you, Jewels. No other women but my sister and my grandmother have ever been in this house. Unless you count my cleaning lady, and she's at least sixty."

Tears trickled. She couldn't stop them. He brushed them away with his warm thumbs. Then, he planted a trail of kisses where her tears had streaked her cheeks. He pulled her close, and she wrapped her arms around his neck as if embracing him were the most natural thing in the world. His lips met hers with feather light caresses. Gradually, he deepened the kiss until her heart pounded in rhythm against his.

He lifted his head and stared into her eyes. With a ragged breath, he said, "I've been waiting a long time to kiss you."

His dark sapphire gaze locked with hers made her forget everything but the two of them. With his arms around her waist, she'd come home at last. "You're an A+ kisser, Officer Walker."

"Not 'D' for developing?"

"Huh?"

"A 'D' means I need more practice."

She giggled. "I need more practice, too."

He kissed her again.

Minutes later, they were sitting down to dinner. He reached across the table for her hand and bowed his head. "Father, thank You for this woman. Until I met Julie, I didn't know how much I missed her."

Her lids flew open then closed again as fast as he offered thanks for their meal. The implication in his words thrilled and unsettled her. When he finished praying, she could barely whisper, "Amen."

What was happening to her? Food was the last thing on her mind. She wanted to ask him about his renewed walk with the Lord, about ... well, everything. She wanted to know everything about him.

No, that wasn't right. She wanted to listen to everything he was willing to share.

Being a cop's daughter, she understood. Some things he would never talk about. Maybe a cop's daughter could make a good wife for a cop after all. Strange, how God worked things out.

She took a long drink of lemonade. "This is homemade isn't it?"

"It is. Glad you like it." Derrick reached for the wedge of parmesan cheese and grated a generous amount on his spaghetti. A thoughtful expression furrowed his brow. "Aren't you going to eat?"

"Of course. Italian food is my favorite." She reached for the spaghetti, served herself a healthy portion, then held her plate out for him to pour the sauce over her pasta.

"How many meatballs do you want, Jewels?"

"Three." Her appetite was back. She was always hungry when she was happy.

Chapter Ten

Between forkfuls of pasta and salad, Derrick glanced at Julie. He couldn't scarcely believe she was here, sitting at his dining table, sharing dinner with him. That kiss, their first kiss, had rocked him to the depths of his soul. He could lose himself in her kisses.

No, that wasn't right. He would find himself in her kisses. And to think he'd believed that the woman for him didn't exist.

As they ate, the silence lengthened. In Derrick's family, dinner had been a time for sharing the day's events. Good conversation was food for the soul and united a family, and he wanted that same unity with Julie. "I forgot to tell you what happened at work Monday night."

She dropped her bread in her lap, snatched it up,

and placed it on her napkin.

He hid his disappointment. *Lord, she can't be scared whenever I'm working.*

Derrick took her trembling hand, but Julie only stared at her lap. "Honey, we have to get something straight right now." He rubbed his thumb over the top of her hand, hoping to soothe her with his touch.

She sighed, then lifted her face to meet his gaze. "Okay."

"God's watching over me. He always has. Even when I was running from Him." Gently, Derrick squeezed Julie's hand. "But I'm not running anymore."

Her lips parted in a soft smile. "I'm glad."

He hesitated. But the rest needed to be said. "Jewels, when I'm working, you have to remember I'm always in God's hands. You have to learn to rest and to trust that God is with me, wherever I go."

She pulled her hand free and absently twirled spaghetti on her fork.

For a moment, he glimpsed the girl she'd been, the girl who'd wrestled at a young age with the knowledge of her dad's mortality. *Father, help her, please.*

With her eyes focused on her plate, Julie whispered, "I'm working on it."

He'd have to be satisfied with that answer. For now.

"So, what happened on Monday night?" she asked, looking up at him.

Tiny frown lines suggested she still wasn't sure she wanted to hear what had happened during his shift. But he needed her to know his job consisted of more than dealing with the dark side of human nature. A resurgence of joy coursed through him at the memory of holding that precious infant girl. "I delivered a baby."

"You did?" Julie beamed at him. "That's awesome."

"It was awesome. God brought Leon and me down the right street at the right time to deliver a baby. A sweet baby girl who might have died if we hadn't been there."

"But you were there." Julie's gaze locked with his.

As he told her the whole story, the wonder of it filled him with reverent thanksgiving. He had participated in the miracle of childbirth, and God had birthed a miracle for Derrick as well. The miracle of at last finding complete peace about his parents' deaths. A silent prayer of thanks soared from his heart.

"I'm so proud of you, Derrick. You're a true hero."

He wanted to tell her God was the true hero. How could he put his new assurance into words? "I was only doing my job."

For several minutes, Julie shared highlights from her day, and Derrick was amazed by her patience, especially with the youngest kids.

When they finished their meal, he said, "You still haven't taken me horseback riding."

She laid her fork on her salad plate. "I'm sorry. I went riding this morning. I take Wednesday mornings off, remember? If I'd known you wanted to go, I would have called you."

He made a mental note. He'd have to take her out for breakfast some Wednesday soon. He couldn't think of a better way to start his day, though it was technically the end of his workday. "Saturday then?"

"Sure."

"I haven't ridden in years. But I'm sure it will all come back to me, especially with you to guide me." He grinned. Though he'd never perfected the art of flirting, he was confident his natural charm communicated his desire to spend as much time with her as possible.

"I'll do my best, but I don't do anything fancy. I ride for pleasure." She picked up her plate, rose from the table, and headed for the sink. Then, she took two steps back and reached around to grab his plate.

Her long hair fell across his face in a floral-scented caress. How much was a man expected to resist? Succumbing, he pulled her onto his lap for a quick kiss. She giggled against his mouth, making it impossible for him to give her the kiss he'd planned.

Pushing against his shoulders, she climbed off his lap, smiled, and waited for him to say something.

"That's good," he said.

Sporting her pink blush, she was enchanting and gorgeous. In fact, every time he kissed her, she looked more beautiful. He was falling as fast as the Niagara River over the Horseshoe Falls, falling deeper in love with her every day.

"What's good?"

"Kissing you."

Her lips parted. But she said nothing.

He recognized his cue to change the subject. "It's also good that you ride your horses for fun. Your schedule is already a bit full. Adding horse training would leave you no time for me."

She laughed then carried their plates and utensils to the sink. Standing with her back to him, she filled the dishpan with soap and hot water. If she were going to wash, he would dry the dishes. His grandfather always helped his grandmother clean up after dinner. Years ago, Derrick had asked why. "Helping your wife is part of romancing her," Grandpa had explained. His grandfather was a wise man. Finding the romance in the ordinary details of life was something Derrick never considered. Until Julie.

He took a clean dish towel from the drawer, but his mind was off drying dishes and on romancing the precious woman next to him before he'd even put away the clean plates, let alone dried the silverware and sorted it into the utensil tray in the drawer. He reached for her hands, removed them from the soapy water, and pulled her into his arms. He brushed a kiss across each flushed cheek and then claimed her mouth. Her lips trembled slightly beneath his. Reining in his emotions, he kept this kiss gentle, sweet, and far shorter than he wanted.

When he lifted his head, the yearning in her soft, blue eyes reminded him of something his father had once said. "The best thing God gives a man other than his salvation is a good wife." He'd been too young at the time to understand what Dad meant. Now Derrick understood.

With her hand on his chest, she asked, "What's wrong?"

His heart raced beneath her fingertips. Her soft floral perfume stirred his senses, nearly eclipsing his judgment. Moving to put some distance between them, he sought to reassure her. "Nothing's wrong, honey. But if we're going to teach Sadie to come from a distance, we better get outside now before it gets dark."

The following morning, Julie arose a full half hour earlier than her usual six a.m. When she entered the kitchen, her father was reading his Bible and drinking coffee. Must be his day off. She couldn't keep track of his schedule, which wasn't surprising. Without her planner and calendar notifications on her phone, she wouldn't be able to keep track of her own.

"Good morning, Dad." She planted a kiss on his smoothly shaved cheek. "How was your night?"

"Pretty crazy for a Wednesday. Especially without one of our best officers."

Julie laughed. "So, Mom told you I had dinner with Derrick last night?"

"Yep. Have fun?"

"Yes, we did."

"Where did he take you?"

She shot her father a look designed to remind him she wasn't in high school anymore. Dad wasn't grilling her. Not really. But she wanted information, too, information only her father would share with her. And she didn't mind making casual conversation about her date if it meant she could find out what she wanted to know.

"Nowhere. He cooked spaghetti and meatballs. After dinner, we trained the dog."

"Doesn't sound too romantic to me. He should have asked me what you like to do."

"I like training dogs."

"Not on a date."

She laughed again, took a loaf of organic bread out of the freezer, and dropped two slices into the toaster. She poured herself a mug of coffee and added chocolate raspberry-flavored creamer. When the toast popped up, she spread a generous amount of peanut butter on both slices before they could cool, drizzled honey on top, and swirled it together with the edge of her knife. Stalling for time, that's what she was doing.

When she'd first thought about dating Derrick, she'd been sure her father would disapprove. Many police officers didn't want their daughters or their sons—though for some archaic reason, *that* was less of an issue—to date other officers.

"Derrick and I had a nice time together." She carried her breakfast to the table and settled in across from her father. "I like him, Dad. A lot."

He folded his hands on the table. "And how exactly does Derrick Walker feel about you?"

His eyes searched hers, probing for what he termed was a satisfactory answer. Her father had always been more protective than other dads. He'd been mad as a pit bull in protection mode when he'd first learned of Nick's betrayal, so Dad's direct question about Derrick's intentions didn't surprise her.

"He likes me, too." *He's nothing like Nick.*

"Are you in love with him?"

She washed down the toast in her mouth with a long swallow of coffee. "I haven't even known the man three weeks. Don't you think it's a little soon to be asking that question?"

"Not at all. I fell in love with your mother the minute I saw her. She claims it took her about a month to be sure about me, but I know better."

Her dad believed in love at first sight? She didn't know him as well as she'd thought. "How did you know?"

"Know what, that I loved your mother, or that she loved me?"

"Both."

"Give me a second, and I'll answer both questions." Dad poured himself another cup of coffee, and paused in the entryway to the front room, watching for Mom, no doubt. For the next five minutes, he shared fond memories of the days before he and her mother were married.

Julie had always believed her parents shared a deep, abiding love. What she had never realized was that his love for his wife was the most important thing in her father's life. More important than being a police officer. All the while she had been terrified of losing her father, he had never once taken unnecessary chances with his life. He had done his job to the best of his ability, always mindful that his family was depending on him to make it home safely every night. If only she'd known all that sooner.

She drained her coffee and looked up to find her dad studying her.

"Are you all right, Julie?"

She rose from her chair, wrapped her arms around his neck, and kissed his cheek. "I love you, Dad."

He stood and gave her a quick hug. "I love you, too, girl."

He gathered their plates and empty coffee mugs from the table then placed them in the sink. "Make sure Walker doesn't break your heart."

"He won't."

"That's good because I don't want to have to drum up some reason to fire one of my best men."

He was kidding, joking around with her to lighten the mood.

But he'd given her the perfect opportunity to ask the question that nagged at her. Asking it almost felt like betrayal, but she couldn't give Derrick the trust he needed from her without the answer. She had to know. "Dad, Derrick's not reckless or hotheaded, is he?"

Her father's eyes filled with tender compassion. "He doesn't take unnecessary chances, but in a dangerous situation, there's no one else Ryan and I would rather have respond to our call for backup."

She released the breath she hadn't realized she'd been holding. Derrick was brave, trustworthy, and cautious, a good combination, and the mark of an excellent cop. She couldn't ask anything more of him. Short of asking him to quit the force. And she wouldn't do that. He shouldn't have to choose between her and his work. *Lord, You promised Your grace is sufficient.*

"Thanks, Dad, for being honest with me. Your good opinion of Derrick means a lot."

Late Thursday night, right before Derrick left for work, Mel called. Bob was suffering with one of his two-day migraines. They'd postponed their flight until Monday, to be sure he'd be over his wicked headache. It had cost them a small fortune, but Bob's migraines were brutal. Not something he could deal with on an airplane. Especially with the changes in cabin pressure on the ascent and descent.

"Not a problem, Sis," Derrick reassured her. "Sadie and I are best friends. We've had no problems. Harmony, obedience, and safety are the rule."

"Sure. Whatever you say," Mel muttered, her tone suggesting she couldn't spare another minute, not even to discuss how Sadie was doing.

In the distance, Bob called for a cold washcloth.

"I have to hang up, Derrick. See you and Sadie on Monday."

"I'll be praying for Bob," Derrick said. But Mel had already hung up.

On Saturday morning, as Derrick pulled up to the barn, Trace Adkins' "You're Gonna Miss This" poured from a radio in the stables. Derrick agreed with the song's message. He intended to appreciate every moment with Julie. Ambling his way up the well-worn dirt path, he took his time watching her groom and saddle up the pretty palomino he'd admired the day Maggie Morrison had shown him Shady Meadows.

But it wasn't the horse that captivated him today. Julie was lovely, lovelier than this idyllic setting that suited her so well. He was glad she'd decided not to sell. She belonged here.

You want to belong here, too. Right beside her, every day.

She glanced over her shoulder and waved. "Hi, Derrick. You're right on time."

The smile illuminating her face made him long to sweep her into his arms and carry her over the threshold of this beautiful home that reminded them both of happy childhood memories. More than that, he was eager to make new memories with her. Starting today.

"Morning, Jewels." He erased the distance between them in two strides. The expectation in her sweet blue eyes, coupled with her parted pink lips sealed his course. He wrapped his arms around her slim waist, eased her against his chest, and slanted his mouth over hers. He brushed her lips, teasing, tasting her berry-flavored sweetness. She linked her hands behind his neck and held him tenderly, possessively. Reluctantly, he ended the kiss but kept her close.

"Hi, beautiful."

"Hi," she said breathlessly.

His kiss had affected her as much as it had him. That knowledge made him want to kiss her again. Made him know he probably should not kiss her again. Because he wanted a lot more than a simple kiss, he released her. But when she stepped out of his embrace, his arms felt empty.

Strategy, man. You want to woo her and give her the wedding of her dreams. Eloping immediately is not an option.

Even if it were, her dad would have Derrick's hide.

Attempting to get his head back in the present, Derrick patted the pretty palomino. "It's a great day for a trail ride."

Julie nodded. "I was thinking, maybe this afternoon,

if you don't already have other plans, we could head over to the park and start teaching Sadie to come from a greater distance."

He nodded, but his mind wasn't on training his dog. Or on riding the horses through Shady Meadow's amazing trails. He was thinking about how long he'd have to wait before he could propose and receive her immediate "yes."

"Are you listening to me?" Her lips puckered in a pout.

Ouch. He was already getting that question? He'd have to stop letting his mind wander. He didn't want to be one of those guys who hardly ever listened to his wife. Funny how he was already thinking of her as his wife. His renewed faith increased his confidence, not because Derrick had it all together, but because he finally believed God was for him and wanted to bless his heart's desire. And his heart's desire was to marry Julie. Before the end of the year. Now, all he had to do was convince her.

"Derrick, I asked you if you wanted to go to the park later and continue training Sadie to come from a distance."

"I heard you. But I'm not sure that's a good idea. I don't think Sadie will come to either of us. Not consistently. And I don't want to chance her running off."

Julie rested her palm on his chest. "We'll train her on a twenty-foot lead. That way she can't run off."

"Sounds safe enough."

"It's settled then." She patted his chest and double-checked the cinches on her horse.

Her certainty should have reassured him, but Derrick still had misgivings. Maybe, if they used a long lead, they could keep Sadie safe. He made it a point to never take any chances where his sister was concerned. He'd been her champion and guardian for so long it was hard to relinquish the job to his new brother-in-law, though Derrick couldn't have found a better husband for his sister had he handpicked the man himself. Except for being allergic to dogs. But that one had worked out in Derrick's favor.

Leaving her horse ground-tied outside the barn door, Julie reentered the stable. He followed behind, wondering which horse she'd chosen for him. Stopping at the stall of an American Paint, she greeted the gelding in soft, soothing tones and stroked his majestic head. The horse responded by nuzzling her hand, and she led the beautiful animal out to the center of the barn and cross-tied him. "I need to clean his hooves, and he can be a bit cranky about it sometimes. It's safer for him, and for me, if I cross-tie him."

"That's the way Mel and I did all our horses. Want some help?"

Julie shook her head. "Comet's funny about his feet. Why don't you stand by his head and let him get used to you? Especially if you want to ride him."

She winked, and her playful grin brought the pink

glow to her cheeks that he loved.

She sure looked kissable. Maybe he could propose over dinner tonight. *Get real, man. You're reacting like a testosterone-driven teenager. You don't have a ring yet.*

"Unless you'd prefer to ride Sunny."

They both burst out laughing. With her small stature, Sunny was a woman's horse. His sister would love her. Hopefully, Mel and Julie would hit it off. Mel had always wanted a sister. At least, that's what she used to tell him when she'd get fed up with his bossy, overprotective ways.

"You ride Sunny, Jewels. Comet and I will get along fine."

In ten minutes, she had saddled up the gelding, and they headed east into the woods that edged Shady Meadows. The scents of pine and some flower he didn't recognize sweetened the air. He had always loved the seasons for their unique gifts, but for years Derrick had been too busy honing his body and mind to enjoy nature. His grandmother complained often that he'd forgotten how to relax. Since his parents' deaths, he'd considered relaxation a luxury reserved for those with fewer responsibilities. But he'd been wrong to shut out the daily joys and comforts God provided. He would have to tell Grandma that the next time he saw her.

"Thank you for sharing this day with me, Jewels." Derrick readjusted his position. His form wasn't what it used to be.

She twisted in her saddle, glanced back at him, and

their eyes met. "My pleasure. How are you doing? You look like a man with a lot on his mind."

"I was wondering what I ever did to deserve this."

She slowed her horse to wait for him to come alongside her. "Deserve what?"

"God's patience and forgiveness. You. Everything."

She pulled back on the reins to stop her horse.

He did the same.

"None of us deserve anything from God," Julie said. "It's all His grace and His mercy."

"I'm thankful for His mercy. But sometimes I think I may have taxed His patience too much. All those years I blamed Him for my parents' deaths, God never abandoned me." Derrick couldn't count the number of times he could have been killed, both in Afghanistan and even out patrolling Buffalo's streets. "Now, I know it was because He still had plans for me. Plans that included meeting you."

Derrick examined her face for any anxiety. He didn't want to move too fast. The peace in her eyes reassured him, and with one hand on the saddle horn for balance, he leaned toward her to kiss her cheek. But she turned her head and met his lips in a sweet kiss interrupted by the stomping of Comet's hooves. They both laughed and signaled their horses to walk on. He could get used to being this happy and content.

❄

By the end of the day, Derrick was ready to tell Julie about the part she'd played in his return to his Shepherd. She didn't know it, but she had given him a great gift.

Under the stars, sitting on her aunt's front porch steps, eating grilled corn and hot dogs, he drank in the sight of the woman he loved. The moonlight shimmered in her blonde hair, and her face wore an expression that was a combination of contentment, satisfaction, and fatigue after a long day well spent. She looked adorable as she wiped butter off her chin.

"Julie, I want to thank you," he began, unsure how to explain.

"Thank me for what? You did all the cooking."

He laughed at the quirky way she wrinkled her nose. He tried to resist the urge to touch her but ended up running his index finger down her nose to her mouth.

She surprised him by kissing his finger.

He let out a ragged breath. Forgetting all about what he wanted to share with her, he leaned over and kissed her, tasting the salt and butter on her lips. She kissed him back like they'd been a couple for months instead of days. With his hands still in her silky hair, he broke off the kiss. "Jewels, I—"

She stopped him with a finger over his mouth. "Not yet, Derrick. I want to wait until ..."

Wait until what? Surely, she didn't think he was suggesting they do anything. He could never disrespect her like that. "Julie, I have no intention of taking advantage of you."

The deep blush staining her cheeks testified to her acute embarrassment. "Oh, I thought …"

He inched away from her to give her space but took her hands in his. "What I was going to say is I'm in love with you."

Her eyes glistened with tears.

Which wasn't the reaction he'd hoped for.

He knew she loved him, too, though she hadn't said the words. That part didn't bother him. His grandmother always said a woman wants a man to declare himself first.

But her tears weren't happy tears.

Eager to set her mind at ease, he said, "I'm not expecting you to tell me yet that you love me." With his thumbs, he rubbed soothing circles on the backs of her hands. "But when you've seen as much death as I have you don't wait to tell someone you love them, because you might not get another chance."

The anguish in her eyes made him want to hold her forever, but she pulled away, hurried up the steps onto the porch, and busied herself with covering the dishes of food.

He followed, at a loss over how to fix everything between them. Putting his hands gently on her waist, he eased her around so she had to look at him. "I know it's hard for you, Jewels, that I'm a cop."

"It's not that, Derrick. At one time, you being a cop

scared me enough to keep me pushing you away despite how attracted I was to you from the moment you walked into Canine Jewels."

He reached for her hand and held it. "Then, why are you upset? Something's wrong. Is this about that guy?"

Her flustered expression told him he'd guessed right.

She pulled her hand free and trudged away from him. "How do you know about him?"

He came up behind her and eased her against his chest, wrapping his arms around her stomach. "Your mom said you'd been hurt once before. At brunch, while you were in the bathroom, your mother wanted to tell me, but your dad wouldn't let her."

Leaning against Derrick for support bolstered her flagging courage. Julie didn't want to face him when she told him what a fool she'd been. "Nick and I were engaged. He wanted me." Her voice was shaking, but she had to tell it all. "In every way. He said it didn't matter to God because we were getting married soon. A lot of girls, even some who had gone to church their whole lives, said waiting to have sex wasn't necessary."

She paused. Why didn't Derrick ask a question— something that would make it easier for her to reveal her shame? *Lord, help me tell him.*

Derrick kissed the top of her head. But he didn't say a word.

"One friend told me a line existed, and if I crossed it, I wouldn't be thinking about my conviction to wait for marriage. I didn't want to get anywhere near that line. Nick kept pressuring me, for months, telling me if I really loved him, I'd trust him. But I wouldn't give in. So, he found another girl who would. I … I found them together."

"That scumbag." Derrick gently pulled her into his arms and lifted her chin until their eyes met. "He didn't deserve you."

"What?"

"He didn't deserve you. If he couldn't respect your convictions, he didn't deserve you."

The love and respect in Derrick's eyes changed everything, opening her mind to the truth. She may have been fooled by Nick's pretending to be a Christian, but ultimately, she had nothing to be ashamed of. She had made the right choice when it counted most.

"What did you do?" Derrick asked. "After you caught him cheating on you?"

A knot of tension uncoiled where she'd hidden the painful memories away, hoping to forget how easily she'd been deceived. Looking back on it now, after all these years, her reaction was hilarious. "I whipped his engagement ring at his face."

"You didn't?"

She giggled. "I did. It hit him smack in the left eye.

That rock gave him a shiner. Our breakup was the talk of the campus for weeks."

Chapter Eleven

Julie got up early to run before church. Running helped her think more clearly. Running in the morning allowed her to connect with Jesus before the day's pressures dulled her hearing. In her experience, the biggest impediment to hearing from the Lord was the constant whirr of thoughts in her own brain. Being outside helped her refocus on God, helped her relinquish her need to figure things out. Immediately. Or better yet, yesterday.

Yesterday, Derrick had told her he loved her. She had a lot to think and pray about.

She chugged half her water, left the bottle on the porch railing, and jogged off. She'd completed her favorite trek through Akron Falls Park and was on her way home before she was finally ready to tell Derrick she loved him, too. Now that she'd told him about Nick, nothing prevented her from revealing her heart to Derrick and trusting God with their future.

A few blocks from home, she slowed to an easy jog. Minutes later, she reached the porch steps, grabbed her water, and drank the rest before going through her cool down stretches. She showered and dressed for church in less than twenty minutes. After a quick cup of coffee and toast with peanut butter, she was in her car driving to church. She popped in her favorite praise and worship CD and tried to prepare her mind for the service. Would she be too excited to sit still?

The church parking lot was packed when she arrived at five minutes before ten o'clock, but Derrick's SUV was nowhere in sight. Walking at a fast clip, she could hardly check each row of vehicles. As she entered the sanctuary, the congregation was on their feet singing, so she couldn't scan the room for Derrick without being obvious. Squelching her disappointment, she took her place next to her father at the end of their pew and opened a songbook, though she knew the words to "Jesus the Light of the World." She closed her eyes, letting the familiar words calm her.

Until spicy aftershave wafted to her nose and Derrick's rich tenor joined her alto.

He captured her hand and gave it a quick squeeze. "Sorry I was late," he whispered as the congregation bowed their heads for the pastor's opening prayer. "Were you worried?"

"Not a bit. God's helping me with that issue."

"That's good, Jewels. I'm glad."

Elderly Mr. Jacobsen turned in his pew and leveled Julie and Derrick with a look reminiscent of the high school principal he'd been for 40 years. She flushed with embarrassment. They'd been acting like teens, whispering back and forth during the prayer.

Lord, help me remember Your timing is perfect. Always. In every situation.

Pastor Steve was continuing his study on the book of Acts. Today, he recounted trial after dangerous trial endured by the Apostle Paul. Even in the face of possible death on the sea, Paul never lost his confidence in God's love and care. Everyone around Paul was terrified their ship would sink, and they would all drown. But he trusted God to protect them. Although the ship ran aground and was broken up by the waves, God provided a way for Paul and all who traveled with him to make it safely to the shore.

This story held a lesson for Julie. For years, her sense of security had come from the people who loved her. It was past time she let Jesus be her peace. Totally. After all, her Lord controlled everything pertaining to her, and He had promised to work out everything in her life for her good! She couldn't begin to comprehend the magnitude of such love, but her thinking shifted to begin to embrace the truth.

Her confidence in herself had wavered often, leaving her feeling insecure and vulnerable. And she'd been afraid to place her confidence in her father. Or in Derrick. Especially in Derrick. If she were ever going to live the full life God planned for her, she would have to start thinking differently. From now on, the foundation for her confidence had to rest in her relationship with her Lord, not with people.

As the congregation bowed their heads for the closing prayers, Julie's old struggle reared its head. Every muscle in her body poised for fight or flight. What would become of her if she lost Derrick or her dad? Her chest tightened. Either one would take part of her heart with him. Knowing was easier than accepting that those she loved may not always be there for her.

Breathe. In. Out. In. Out.

Be still. I will never leave you or forsake you.

Her pulse slowed. She unclenched her hands. She could count on God when she couldn't count on herself, her father, or Derrick.

Lord, I do believe You know what's best for me. Help me to trust Your plan for me and Derrick. Your plans are more wonderful than anything I could ask for or imagine. I choose to believe Your Word, no matter what I'm thinking or feeling.

Your plans are more wonderful ... "Wonderful, wonderful, Jesus is to me ..."

The silent song filled every corner of her spirit, chasing away her fears. She could scarcely keep her feet from dancing before the Lord. What would Derrick think if she ran through the aisles shouting hallelujah, thank You, Jesus?

Gradually, her spirit quieted. She opened her eyes to find Derrick studying her.

"You okay?"

She smiled, nodded, and reached to take his hand. How could she express the sheer joy of walking for the first time in expectation of abundant life?

That evening, Derrick called to ask Julie to keep Sadie overnight. His cleaning lady absolutely refused to work with the German shepherd in the house, crated or not. The one time Sally had cleaned since he'd gotten the dog, Derrick had managed to arrange his schedule so he could be home. He wanted to give Sally the opportunity to get used to Sadie, but the woman's childhood fear of big dogs made that difficult. His original plan to be home again tomorrow had fallen through when he'd learned he had to be in court all morning. If Julie couldn't keep Sadie, Sally wouldn't be able to clean for another two weeks because her full schedule precluded the possibility of an alternate date any time this week.

Unfortunately, the kennels at Julie's Canine Jewels were all occupied by other boarders. And her mother was having the carpets shampooed in the morning, so Julie couldn't bring the dog to her parents' house. A German shepherd traipsing over damp cream-colored rugs wouldn't be a pretty sight. At Derrick's suggestion, Julie agreed to board Sadie at the farm, though she disliked the idea of the dog being out there alone. Derrick's solution was for Julie to sleep overnight at Shady Meadows with the dog. Since she'd be moving out to the farm soon, his suggestion was reasonable.

Julie pulled into her driveway at nine-thirty. She parked next to Derrick's SUV in front of the barn, but he and Sadie weren't waiting in the vehicle.

A moment later, the pair rounded the southwest corner of the barn. Julie took great satisfaction in the easy pace he was setting for the shepherd who walked step-to-step on the man's right side. All their hard work had paid off. "Nice form."

Derrick grinned. "We have a great teacher."

"Great teachers can't teach at all without willing students."

He pulled her into his arms. "Then, allow me to teach you how I want you to greet me." He kissed her.

She giggled.

"How am I supposed to kiss you properly if you're laughing? I can see we're going to need a lot more practice."

"Derrick Walker, stop flirting with me. We need to get Sadie settled in for the night."

He narrowed his eyes. "Eager to get rid of me?"

"Of course not." She squirmed in his arms, and he released her. "The kennel is on the east side of the barn."

Illuminated by the security light on the pole in front of the barn, the weathered kennel looked sound enough, but Aunt Elaine and Uncle Fred's beagle had passed away years ago, and the space hadn't been used since. Julie unlatched the gate and yanked the door free from the tall grass tangled in the chain-link fencing.

Derrick and Sadie paused at the entrance. The dog dug in her nails and resisted their attempts to encourage her to check out her temporary quarters. Impatient, Derrick lifted the suspicious canine in his arms, deposited her inside, and hurried out the door before she could follow. Sadie barked at him, declaring her acute displeasure.

"She'll quiet down in a few minutes." He knelt in front of the door and stroked Sadie by poking his fingers through the chain-link fence. "You'll be all right, girl. I promise. It's one night."

Julie shook her head. Her experience told her the shepherd would bark off and on most of the night. "Why don't I bring her inside? She can sleep on the floor next to my bed."

He looked up from his kneeling position. "Would you really do that? I'm sure she would be good."

"I'll have to put her out here when I leave for work in the morning." Aunt Elaine had beautiful antique furniture, and Derrick hadn't been able to break Sadie of her chewing habit yet. She might be good in the house. She might not. Julie didn't want to risk it. Trying to ignore the vague anxiety gnawing at her mind, she asked, "What time can you come out and get her?"

"I'll be done in court at noon." He unlatched the kennel door, reattached Sadie's lead to her collar, and patted her head. "You win this time, girl. You get to sleep in the house."

Julie chuckled. "You talk like you believe she was manipulating you."

"She wasn't?" He swatted a mosquito on his bare arm.

Probably the same mosquito she'd missed when she'd slapped her ankle moments before. "Dogs don't strategize."

"All females strategize—"

"Derrick!"

"I'm teasing you."

She harrumphed. "So, you'll get here about—"

"Sally will be finished cleaning by one o'clock. How about meeting me out here for a picnic lunch around one-thirty?"

Julie smiled, her worries about Sadie eclipsed by her anticipation of enjoying a picnic with Derrick. She had to stop herself from shaking her head. She had never imagined she would be the kind of woman who wanted to see her boyfriend every day. "Sounds good. Whoever gets here first will let Sadie out of the kennel."

Halfway to the house, Julie said, "You know, we've been seeing each other almost every day." In the combined light of the security lamp, the crescent moon, and the spattering of stars, she suspected he could see her blushing. Drat. Why did God have to make her so fair?

When they reached the front porch, he said, "I'm not complaining. Are you?"

She shook her head. "Not a bit."

He motioned for Sadie to lie at their feet. "Down, girl." The shepherd obeyed instantly.

Derrick held his arms out to Julie, and she stepped into his embrace. He brushed a quick kiss across her lips. She molded her body to his and lifted her face for a proper kiss, but he only cradled her head in the curve of his neck, so she wrapped her arms tightly around his waist and let the beating of his heart soothe her.

"Tired?" he murmured against her hair.

"A little. You?"

"It was a long weekend. I should head home."

Reluctantly, she stepped out of his arms.

He smiled, patted Sadie's head, and kissed Julie's cheek. "Goodnight. I'll see you both tomorrow."

"Goodnight."

She watched from the porch with Sadie sitting beside her knee as Derrick turned his SUV around and headed down the long driveway. Fifteen minutes later, Julie had brushed her teeth, donned her pajamas, and settled the dog on the braided rug next to her bed. When her cell phone rang, she figured Derrick was probably calling to say goodnight again.

"Hi, honey. I forgot to tell you, your dad and I had a good talk this afternoon."

A good talk? What did that mean? Had he talked with her dad about marrying her? "What did he say? What did you say?"

"Let's just say we understand each other."

She wiped her sweaty palms on the faded comforter, took a deep calming breath, and decided against asking Derrick for details. For once in her life, she would *not* try to control things, no matter how nervous she felt. "Thanks for letting me know you talked to Dad."

They said goodnight, and she decided to read a few Psalms before she switched off the light. Each one emphasized the importance of trusting God. Trust God when you are afraid. Trust Him when you are confused or in trouble. Trust Him in every situation because He has everything under control. She had read those same verses many times before, but tonight the truth struck a much deeper chord.

"You've got to be kidding me," Derrick moaned, panic laced in his tone.

Julie swallowed hard to keep from crying. "I don't how she got out. The latch is still locked." The answer hit her with a wave of nausea. Sadie had climbed over the eight-foot kennel fence.

"Have you called dog control yet?"

"I called them first."

"Okay. I'm about ten minutes from the farm. Wait

for me, and we'll look for her together."

Disconnecting the call, Julie fell to her knees in the grass in front of the closed kennel door. "Lord, please don't let anything happen to Sadie. I couldn't bear it. Protect her and help us to find her quickly."

Ninety minutes later, they still hadn't found Sadie. As Derrick and Julie fought their way through the dense underbrush in the woods beyond the kennel, he was beginning to think they would be more successful making up posters with Sadie's picture and putting them up in East Aurora and along the route to his house in Lancaster. Julie's strained expression and the determined, frenzied way she hacked through tangled branches and weeds with the sharp sickle made him more worried about her by the minute. "Honey, let's take a break."

"Take a break? When we have no idea how long she's been gone?" Her shoulders shook, and she swiped the tears from her face. "She could be anywhere! She could be hurt, and it's all my fault."

He urged her into his arms, hoping to calm her. "It's not your fault. Neither of us could have known Sadie was such a great climber."

She pushed him away, refusing his comfort. "*I* should have known," she insisted. "I should have been prepared. It's my job to keep dogs safe."

The haunted look in her eyes ripped through him. Something more than Sadie missing was torturing Julie. *Lord, help me help her, please. I can't stand to see her hurting like this.*

"Julie, you can't be everywhere. You're one woman doing her best to teach dog owners how to protect their dogs, and you're great at your job. But you can't keep every dog safe."

A stricken expression settled on her pale face. "I couldn't even protect my own dog."

He stared at her. So that's why she was so passionate about her work. She had lost a beloved pet. "Do you want to tell me about it?"

Julie remembered screaming, "Toby! No!"

The screech of the pickup truck's tires and her own anguished cries thundered in her ears. In bare feet and pajamas, she raced to the pup's side. Toby was lying on the gravel where he'd been thrown by Dad's truck. Was he moving? *Oh, God, please.* She dropped to her knees, gently lifted her sweet puppy onto her lap, and stared with horror as he struggled to breathe. She was powerless to help him. He was dying, and it was all her fault. Sobs wracked her body as she fought the nausea burning her throat.

Julie forced her thoughts back to the present. The memory of that terrible morning was so vivid, the pain razor-sharp. She was a grown woman. Toby had died 17 years ago. *Father, help me get past my grief.*

Derrick touched her shoulder. The tender concern in his eyes soothed her scarred heart.

"When I was ten, I had a yellow lab puppy named Toby." Surprised at how easy it was to share her sorrow with this man she loved so much, she said, "Toby was killed because I let him sneak past me out the front door. I'd heard Mom pacing and praying for Dad off and on all night. Something was up, and I was scared and worried. In the morning, when Dad finally pulled in the driveway, I sprinted outside without thinking. And Toby raced in a yellow blur toward the road. It was so foggy Dad never saw him. I called him, over and over, but Toby wouldn't come to me."

Derrick opened his arms, and she accepted the safe circle he offered. "Honey, it's okay to cry. You need to let this out."

She shook her head. "Crying doesn't change things."

But she knew she was wrong. Her tears mattered to God. *Lord, forgive me for slipping back into my old ways, for reacting rather than responding to this situation. I trust You, Lord. I know You'll help us find Sadie.*

With one finger, Derrick lifted her chin until their faces were inches apart. "You're right, Julie, crying doesn't change things. Crying changes you. After my parents died, my grandmother told Mel and me that crying makes you ready to let the Lord love you again.

You let the tears out, and then, you can let Him in."

Julie had hidden her grief over Toby's death behind hard work and a cheerful smile. But now she was ready to let it all go. She wept on Derrick's shoulder, soothed by his strong arms about her. *Lord, help me forgive myself for Toby's death.*

And with that one prayer, the Lord lifted the burden of guilt she had carried needlessly for seventeen years.

"You were a little girl." Derrick caught her gaze and held it. "You didn't mean to let Toby out. And you didn't mean for Sadie to get out either. Sometimes, accidents happen that are beyond our control."

"Like your parents?"

"Yes. Like my parents."

He cradled her, his head leaning on hers for several minutes as she listened to his heart's steady rhythm.

Derrick released her and took her hand in his. "I think we should pray."

With a surge of renewed hope, she nodded.

"Lord, we need Your help finding Sadie. We don't know where to look, but You know where she is. Please keep her safe until we find her. Amen."

He sounded so confident Julie half-expected to see Sadie bounding toward them the moment they opened their eyes. But another hour passed with no evidence of the dog.

"Julie, we have to head back. It's three o'clock, and we both need to eat."

She didn't want to stop searching, but he was right.

They had walked for miles, through Shady Meadows land and several yards into the neighboring farms. Bent and broken branches and underbrush suggested the presence of deer, but Derrick and Julie hadn't been able to track the dog. "Okay, let's take a break. I forgot our sandwiches in my car, and all I have at the farm is bread and eggs."

He smiled. "That's good enough for me. We'll eat, make up posters with Sadie's picture, and hang them up between here and my house. We'll stop at the shops in East Aurora, too."

After a fast meal of scrambled eggs and toast, they headed over to her school to use her computer. By six-thirty, they had tacked up twenty posters on telephone poles between South Wales and Lancaster along Derrick's usual route. And they'd left posters with a dozen shop owners in East Aurora.

They were heading back to the farm when Derrick's cell phone rang.

He said hello, and Julie willed the caller to be someone who had found Sadie. Or at least someone who had seen her. *Please, God, let her be okay. Surely someone's found her by now.*

His face paled. "Melanie, hi."

Julie couldn't make out what his sister was saying, but Derrick was smiling now. "Thank God," he said into the cell. Then, he whispered, "One of your neighbors called Mel. Mrs. Daniels has Sadie."

Julie wept joyful tears. "Thank You, Lord."

"Mel and Bob are still at the airport, so we need to pick up Sadie."

The second he said goodbye to his sister, Julie asked, "Was your sister mad?"

"No. She was a little shook up, but mostly she was glad someone had found Sadie. Mrs. Daniels got Mel's number off Sadie's name tag. I can't believe I never thought to get a new tag made." Momentary guilt dimmed his eyes.

"You'll get one made tomorrow."

He nodded. "Mrs. Daniels told Mel Sadie came right to her, the first time she called for her to come."

"Thank goodness we worked on that command. Sadie's a fast learner."

"She had two good teachers." Derrick pulled Julie close for a hug. He looked into her tear-filled eyes. "I'd say we make an amazing team. Wouldn't you?"

She wrapped her arms around his neck and kissed him.

Other than the burdock tangled in her tail, Sadie looked fine. She bounded straight for Derrick, put her paws up on his chest, and licked his face.

"Thank you, Mrs. Daniels," Julie said. "I don't know what we would have done if you hadn't spotted Sadie trying to get into your garbage can."

Mrs. Daniels brushed her snow-white hair off her

forehead and sighed. "I'm grateful she didn't get into that can. Samuel and I had fried chicken for supper last night, and if Sadie got a chicken bone caught in her throat … The good Lord was looking out for your dog."

Derrick and Julie agreed. "Yes, He was."

"We'd like to take you and your husband out to dinner to thank you," Derrick said.

They were thinking alike already? Like some old, married couple who knew each other's thoughts?

Whoa, Julie, don't get ahead of God. Or Derrick. He hasn't proposed yet.

"That's not necessary," Mrs. Daniels was saying. "But Samuel and I were about to have supper, and we'd be pleased if you two would join us."

Having her neighbor think Julie and Derrick were a couple made her smile. "Thank you, but we actually ate a late lunch."

After thanking Mrs. Daniels again, Derrick hooked the leash to Sadie's collar. "Come on, girl. Let's get you home where you belong."

They promised Mrs. Daniels they'd come over for supper on Thursday night. Then, Derrick helped Julie and Sadie into the SUV, and headed down the road toward Shady Meadows. "I need to take Sadie home and shower before work."

Familiar anxiety crept into Julie's mind. The stress of the day was taking its toll. If only he didn't have to work tonight. Surely, he couldn't be at his best on the streets after searching all day for Sadie.

"I'll call you in the morning." He reached across the console to squeeze her hand. "So, you won't have to worry about me."

"Okay." She tried to dismiss her concerns. "But don't forget, because I'll be up early waiting for your call."

Parked in front of the barn, he leaned over and kissed the tip of her nose. "I promise I'll call about seven-thirty. You can count on it."

Julie jerked awake.

The telephone was ringing in the hallway outside her bedroom. She reached for the clock radio and yanked it toward her. "Two-thirty!"

She bolted from the bed. Switched on the light. Grabbed her cell phone. Flipped it open. No missed calls. Suffocating dread swept through her. No one would call this late. Unless ...

She raced into the hall, expected to find her mother talking on that phone. But the hallway was empty. Julie froze. Something awful had happened. Fear gripped her with viselike force.

God, please.

When her mother opened the master bedroom door, the stricken look on her face confirmed Julie's worst fears.

Jesus, please. Not Dad.

Julie's head was spinning. She would faint if she didn't sit down. But she ran to her mother. "Is Dad all right?"

Mom gripped Julie's shoulders. "Dad's fine."

"But something's happened. I can see it in your eyes."

Mom's hands trembled, and Julie's shoulders shook, too. "Tell me. Tell me what's happened."

"It's Derrick, Julie. He … he took a bullet meant for your father. Derrick's in surgery."

"No. It can't be him. You're wrong. It must be somebody else. Somebody who—"

"Honey, that was Dad on the phone. Derrick saved his life. Dad's waiting at ECMC with several officers from the precinct. The hospital has already notified Derrick's sister and his grandparents."

A strangled cry erupted from Julie's throat. This couldn't be happening. Not now. She slumped to the floor and wept.

How long she had been crying. A minute? Ten minutes? Her mother was stroking her hair and whispering. Something. But what? Julie couldn't make her brain focus on Mom's words.

Derrick could be dying, and she had never told him she loved him.

It was happening exactly as he had said. "When you've seen as much death as I have, you don't wait to tell someone you love them, because you might not get another chance." His words echoed like an indictment in her head. She might not get another chance.

"Julie, get dressed," her mother urged. "I'll take you to the hospital."

Julie swiped at her eyes with the back of her hand. She struggled to her feet. How long had she been sitting like a crumpled rag doll when her chance to tell Derrick how much she loved him could be slipping away?

Nauseated by the bleakness of a future without him, she raced to her room and pulled on the same clothes she had worn earlier.

Everything felt wrong. Surreal.

Like when Dad's truck struck Toby and threw him three feet into the air, only to come crashing to the ground with a terrible thud.

Please, Lord, don't let Derrick die. I love him so much. He needs to know I love him. Please let me be able to tell him.

Mom had the engine running when Julie reached the car. She climbed in the passenger side. Thank goodness her mother was driving. Julie couldn't trust herself to concentrate long enough to make the twenty-five-minute drive to Erie County Medical Center.

A thick fog shrouded the country roads leading to the 33 Expressway. If only there were more streetlights. Odd, how everything seemed so much more possible in the light. If the sunrise would only hurry up. If God would be merciful.

If only Derrick hadn't gone into work tonight.

No, not that. Then, her father would be dead.

Feeling overwrought, Julie kicked off her shoes, pulled her legs up, and hugged her knees to her chest. She wanted to weep, to scream, to wake up from this nightmare. *Jesus, help me. Please. I feel like my mind is about to snap. Take away the fear.*

Julie sucked in a deep breath then let it out. She remembered a Bible verse. "Weeping may endure for a night, but joy cometh in the morning." She'd rejected that verse when her aunt died, but now, Julie clung to it like a lifeline. *Help me, Father. Keep me grounded in Your love.*

Her heart slowed to an even rhythm. "Mom, can you drive faster?"

"We'll be there soon, honey." Mom kept her eyes on the road, though the fog had thinned out in spots. The car's headlights cast an eerie glow on the dips and sharp curves of the road. "About twenty-five more minutes, what with this fog."

"I'm so scared, Mom. Derrick doesn't know I love him."

Mom lifted one hand off the wheel and reached across the seat to squeeze Julie's hand. "That's not true. Derrick does know you love him."

Julie swallowed hard, ignoring the tightness returning to her chest and the flip-flopping in her stomach. "How? I've never told him how I feel."

"Derrick pulled your father aside on Sunday afternoon. 'Don't worry, Detective Barnes,' he said. 'This is the real thing. I love your daughter. She may not be ready to admit it, but she loves me, too.' That's how I know Derrick knows you love him."

Tears streamed down Julie's face. *Lord, please let me be able to tell him. I shouldn't have waited so long to tell him.*

If only she could turn back the clock. *God, You're a God of second chances. And third and fourth …*

"We're all afraid sometimes, honey." Mom glanced at Julie.

They were waiting for the light at Genesee and Transit to turn green. Seconds seemed like minutes.

"But fear strangles faith. That's why we need to pray, so we can have courage and remember God loves our loved ones even more than we do."

Julie studied Mom's lined face. Why had she never noticed before how brave her mother was?

The quiet strains of Debussy's *Claire de Lune* filled the car, and Julie reached to shut the radio off. The news would be on in a moment, and she couldn't bear to hear about a wounded Buffalo Police officer. Because tonight the man who had taken a bullet belonged to her.

Chapter Twelve

If they didn't hear something soon, Julie would go crazy. Her parents were sitting on either side of her, offering what support they could. She was grateful for their prayers. Prayer kept her from racing down the hall toward the operating room, banging on the door, demanding information like a crazy person. Any information. She needed to be patient. But being patient would be so much easier if someone would come out and tell her how Derrick was doing.

Where was the verse in Romans about waiting and hoping for something one couldn't see? Julie flipped through her mom's Bible but failed to locate the verse. Finding it impossible to concentrate, she closed her eyes to pray. It didn't matter whether her prayers were coherent or not. God understood. He had promised to never leave her or forsake her.

No matter what happened after tonight, Julie would love Derrick forever. Whether he was always a cop or not. No matter how much danger he put himself into she wanted to be waiting for him. She wanted to be the one he came home to. Whatever he had to face, she would face, too, with God's help.

Everything would be different from this moment on. She refused to be bound by fear ever again. She was determined to embrace the life she was born to live. She would meet every challenge with God's Word, and He would give her peace because she would choose to trust Him always.

Julie could hardly wait to show Derrick how she had changed. But first she needed to tell him she loved him.

Lifting her head up from her father's shoulder, Julie shifted her position. Her neck, shoulders, and lower back ached. She must have fallen asleep. Sunlight flooded the waiting room. It was after eight o'clock.

The hospital's antiseptic smell was masked by the strong perfume of an elderly lady who was quietly weeping in the far corner of the room. A distinguished gentleman was holding her hand and murmuring consoling words. A dark-haired young woman with shoulder length hair was sleeping with her head on a blond man's shoulder.

They all looked familiar. Where had Julie seen them before? Usually she had no trouble remembering a face, even if she'd only met the person once. That was it. She hadn't met them. She had seen their pictures, on Derrick's living room wall.

Melanie opened her eyes, and Bob nodded at Julie and spoke in a low voice to his wife. Was Mel as protective of Derrick as he was of her?

Unsure of Melanie's approval, Julie approached Derrick's grandparents first. "Mr. and Mrs. Walker?" The older couple studied her for a moment.

His grandfather rose and extended his hand. "You must be Julie."

"Yes, I'm Julie Barnes." She shook his hand. "And you're Derrick's grandparents."

"We are," the lady said, "but we're Mr. and Mrs. O'Neil, his mother's parents." She waved her blue-lined hand in the direction of the younger couple. "And this is Derrick's sister, Melanie, and her husband, Bob."

Remembering her folks, who remained seated on the opposite side of the waiting room, Julie nodded in their direction. "These are my parents, Elizabeth and Tom Barnes."

After exchanging handshakes and courteous greetings, all seven of them grew silent. Another hour inched by before a female doctor in scrubs strode purposefully into the room. The middle-aged woman's strained features revealed her exhaustion, but she was smiling. "Which one of you is next of kin to Derrick

Walker?"

Julie wanted to jump up and shout, *I am*, but she didn't have that right. Yet.

"I'm his grandfather," Mr. O'Neil replied, pulling his wife close to his side, "and this is his grandmother. And his sister and brother-in-law."

"I'm Dr. Gabrielle Lawrence. I performed the surgery on your grandson."

Julie couldn't wait another second. "But how is he? Is Derrick all right? The surgery took so long."

Her father placed his hand on her shoulder. He extended his other hand to the doctor. "I'm Detective Barnes, and this is my daughter, Julie, Officer Walker's girlfriend."

After shaking her father's hand, the doctor explained the details of the surgery in a blur of obscure terms that exacerbated Julie's frustration. Finally, the doctor said, "He'll be in recovery for another forty-five minutes or so. Then, he'll be transferred into surgical intensive care. Family members will be allowed to visit two at a time."

Julie clasped her hand over her mouth. A strangled sob escaped. She didn't care who saw her crying or what they thought of her. This was awful! She wouldn't be able to see Derrick until he was moved to a regular room. Because she was not family.

Mrs. O'Neil slipped her arm around Julie's shoulders and pulled her close. "You'll go in with me, sweetheart." The older woman's voice soothed like the sound of a mother comforting an agitated child. Or a distraught twenty-seven-year-old.

Julie searched the woman's face. "Really?"

"Of course. Don't you worry a bit. My husband will take care of everything."

And he did. Less than an hour later, after Derrick's grandparents, sister, and brother-in-law had all seen him, Julie was seated beside the head of Derrick's bed. She stroked his feverish brow and silently prayed. Her prayers were more like breathing than putting her thoughts into words. With every breath she took, with every beat of her heart, she asked God to infuse her strength into Derrick, and to take his pain and give it to her.

"Julie." Derrick's voice was low and scratchy.

But it was the sweetest sound she'd ever heard. "I'm here."

"Jewels?"

Being careful not to disturb the many wires and tubes that seemed to be connected to every part of him, Julie leaned close to his mouth so she could hear him better. "I'm here, Derrick."

"Sorry ... I ... didn't ... call."

She straightened to look at his dear face and laid her finger over his cracked lips. "Hush. Don't try to talk. You need to rest. Concentrate on getting better."

"Honey, is ... your dad ... okay?"

"Dad's fine. One bullet grazed his left arm, but he's okay." Tears slipped down her cheeks, but she didn't bother to wipe them away. "Because of you, Derrick. You saved his life."

"Had to," Derrick said with obvious struggle.

"Don't try to talk anymore. Not yet." She dipped a washcloth into a small basin of cool water, bathed his face, and kissed his forehead. Leaning close to his ear and hoping her declaration would speed his recovery, she whispered, "I love you, Derrick Walker. And I always will."

But Derrick had drifted back to sleep.

Accepting that she would have to wait a little longer to tell him how much she loved him, Julie settled herself into the cozy armchair. She intended to stay all day. If the nurses didn't kick her out. Hopefully, they would forget she was here.

If she had anything to say about it, Derrick wouldn't wake up without seeing her beside him.

A week later Derrick's neck and left shoulder still ached where he had taken the bullets. He'd been shot twice. The damage to Derrick's shoulder had required extensive repair to the muscles, tendons, ligaments, bones, and joint cartilage. The other bullet had narrowly missed his carotid artery. How it had missed the nerves and vertebrae in his neck only God knew. Derrick believed in bulletproof vests, but he believed in angels more. He had seen too many men cheat death not to believe angels often acted as a shield no human being could explain.

He didn't need to understand *how* God had preserved his life. His grandfather's words the day Derrick had left for Afghanistan resounded in his mind. "When you trust God, you're as safe on the battlefield as you are at home in your own bed, because your life is in God's hands. You remember that, whenever you're in danger. Having courage doesn't mean you're never afraid. Courage is doing what's right, what you have to do, in spite of your fears." Risking his life to protect Julie's dad had been the right thing to do, though Derrick would have done the same for any fellow officer.

Father, thank You for watching over us both. For Julie's sake. And for ours.

Derrick reached for his cell phone to check the time. It was twelve-seventeen. Where was she? She should have been here by now. He inhaled a deep breath and slowly released it. Displaying any irritation with her would be completely unfair.

Every day for the past week, she'd stopped in to visit him sometime between eleven-thirty and noon, bringing different sandwiches from their favorite deli. She had smuggled in cappuccinos in a multitude of flavors for them to try. She had read to him from the Bible, her favorite poets, dog training articles, country living magazines, James Patterson's latest mystery, all to distract Derrick, first from the pain, and later, from his frustration with being confined to the hospital while she moved herself, her belongings, and Sadie out to Shady Meadows. All without his help.

Being confined to a hospital room was chaffing. Especially for a man who had always been able to count on his body doing whatever he needed it to do. Derrick had spent hours studying his Bible and perusing the stack of devotionals his grandfather had discreetly left on the nightstand when he'd thought Derrick was asleep. He'd kept his mind active, but his body had been idle far too long. He was eager to resume some semblance of his normal activities, though he knew he had weeks of physical therapy ahead. And that wouldn't begin until after the bones healed.

He might not be much physical help to the woman he loved, but he'd offer what moral support he could. Erasing the stress that had lined her features since he'd been shot was his top priority. He'd be out of work for at least three months, maybe longer.

Strange, but that didn't bother him much. Being out on disability meant he could focus on Julie and their future together. They had plans to make. Plans he wanted to set in motion today.

For starters, he hoped to persuade her they were partners on every level. With him stuck in a hospital bed, she'd been implementing plans without him. And except for her friend, Stacey, no one was helping Julie. Between running Canine Jewels, exercising the horses, fixing up Shady Meadows, and caring for Sadie, Julie was wearing herself out, and that was unacceptable.

His formidable and tenderhearted woman had even redesigned the old beagle kennel so their beloved Sadie could never climb out again. Julie had stretched and tied chicken wire across the entire top of the kennel. All by herself. How she'd managed on her own was beyond him. She had taken the shepherd out to the farm on the day of his surgery and kept her crated inside until she'd succeeded in making the kennel shepherd-proof. It was the only reasonable solution. That's what Julie had told him the following morning. Sadie couldn't stay alone at Derrick's place, and she couldn't stay with Mel and Bob. Staying at the farm until Derrick was released from the hospital was the best option for Sadie.

After spending over a week in the hospital, he was more than ready to go home. He missed the comfort of the dog's unconditional love, a love he never would have experienced if it hadn't been for Julie. From the moment he and Sadie entered Julie's Canine Jewels, none of their lives had been the same. Looking back, he could see the Lord's hand over and over again. Both Julie and Sadie had been instrumental in helping Derrick find his way back to the man he was always meant to be. The man his parents had raised him to be.

A man who couldn't imagine his life without his two favorite girls.

He strode to the door and peered out of his room, past the nurse's station, and down the hallway. Where was Julie? He shrugged. To kill time, he searched his room, double-checking to ensure he had not forgotten any personal items. Then, he looked at his watch for the umpteenth time. "Twelve-thirty?"

On cue, Julie burst into his room. "Today's the day. You're finally going home. Are you ready to get out of here?"

He grinned. "Definitely." The velvet box with his mother's engagement ring, resized to fit his bride-to-be, thanks to a little help from his sister and the dear lady he hoped would soon be his mother-in-law, lay deep in his pants pocket. The pressure of it against his leg brought a surge of joy, and he tapped down his eagerness.

Stay with the plan, Walker.

He rose from the bed and held out his right arm to Julie. His left arm and shoulder remained encased in a sling designed to keep the joint as immobile as possible. Not being able to hug her with both arms bothered him more than he wanted to admit to her. "Aren't you going to give me a real hug?"

She stood a foot away from him, her expression uncertain.

"You won't hurt me. But don't wrap your arms around my neck the way you like to do and be careful with my shoulder, and I'll be fine."

She released a half-chuckle and inched close with the gentleness of a butterfly lighting on a leaf.

His heart soared at the love shining in her eyes as she gazed up at him. He slipped his good arm around her waist, and she rested her cheek against his chest.

"You have no idea how often I dream of doing this. Thinking about holding you, kissing you, running my fingers through your beautiful hair kept me from being the grouchiest patient on record."

She lifted her face. A sheen of tears in her eyes marred the moment. Her lingering fear was palpable.

"Honey, I'm fine. God was watching over me and your dad the whole time. You know that, don't you?"

She nodded. But her lower lip quivered so slightly he almost missed it.

"I love you, Derrick."

She had said it every day since the accident, usually several times. Before he'd met Julie, Derrick hadn't realized how lonely and parched his life had become. All those long years of running from God and keeping everyone but his family at a safe distance had dulled his self-awareness. Now, Derrick basked in Julie's love, love he returned with every fiber of his being.

"I love you, too. Jewels." He grinned and winked at her. "I'm going to sit down on this bed so you can give me a proper kiss hello."

She complied, but the kiss was too brief, too gentle, too sweet. He wanted more than a sweet kiss. Later. Passionate kisses would come later. After he revealed his plan for his first day home.

Her plan was to drive him out to the farm to pick up Sadie. They would share a quiet, late lunch together, after which she intended to take him and the dog directly home so he could rest. But sleeping was the farthest thing from his mind.

The knots in his gut that had begun when he first opened his eyes that morning twisted again. His ability to master his emotions served him well. No matter how eager he was to set their new life in motion, Derrick's plan did not include proposing in a hospital room. Never mind how the need to put his ring on her finger sent his adrenaline surging. He wanted to create a romantic memory they'd treasure for the rest of their lives.

Shady Meadows was the perfect place to ask Julie to be his wife.

Julie worried and prayed over Derrick as she navigated through the lunch-hour traffic on the expressway heading out of the city. Traffic thinned out as they passed the airport, but he still hadn't said a word. Why was he so quiet? He was probably in more pain than he was letting on. To Derrick, self-discipline meant toughing it out. On more than one occasion, she'd seen him accept the minimum amount of pain relievers, often ignoring the nurses' explanations about windup. "Take the meds and knock the pain out before it winds up to such a high level in the brain that the meds can't touch it. Because then we'll have to increase the dose." But Derrick scoffed at their advice. He wasn't the best patient. And he'd seen firsthand what relying on painkillers could do to a person.

"You okay?" Julie glanced away from the road for a few seconds to search Derrick's features for signs of discomfort.

"I'm fine," he insisted, his blue eyes sparkling with mischief.

What on earth was the man thinking? She raised her eyebrows.

"I'm enjoying being with you. That's all I need."

"Thanks. I enjoy your company, too."

He must be up to something, but what? If she'd just gotten out of the hospital after more than a week, she would need to talk. No one would be able to shut her up. Every few miles, she looked over at him to make sure he was doing okay. His eyes were closed. Was he sleeping? Maybe he was praying. Whatever the cause, he was deep in thought about something.

By the time she pulled into her driveway and parked the car next to the front porch, she felt like she'd bust a vein if he didn't share what he'd been thinking about.

But Sadie had obviously heard the car. She was barking, demanding to be released from the kennel. Before Julie could react, Derrick had managed to get himself out of her car and was opening the driver's side door. How could a man with his injuries move so fast? Because his legs were perfectly fine. Still, shouldn't he be more careful with his shoulder?

"Stop frowning at me, Jewels. I'm not an invalid."

"Okay." She prayed for patience. He was a grown

man. He knew what his body could do. "Let's go get Sadie."

"Not yet." He leaned in close, backing her up against the closed car door. His expressive eyes darkened to a deep blue.

The intensity of his gaze captivated and captured her, driving from her mind all thoughts but him and this moment together. She waited. And waited. "Are you going to kiss me or not?"

He obliged her with an intensity that almost blocked out Sadie's insistent barking. Almost.

The shepherd barked a loud greeting until Julie and Derrick broke off their kiss and hurried to the kennel. Sadie was standing on her hind legs, her front paws on the fence. Delight at seeing Derrick animated the shepherd's soft brown eyes. He put his hand on the chain-link door so the dog could lick his fingers. "She's glad to see me."

"That's what I'm afraid of." Julie attempted to level him with a stern, don't-you-dare-argue-with-me look. "I don't want her jumping on you."

"She won't."

"She will. She's too excited. Go wait on the front porch, and I'll bring her to you on her leash."

He agreed. Too quickly. Something was definitely up.

In a few minutes, she accomplished her goal and marched Sadie up the porch steps to where Derrick waited on the porch swing. "Sadie, sit-stay," Julie commanded.

The dog sat on Derrick's left side and rested her head on his knee. What a smart dog she was to realize her master needed protection on that side.

He reached across his lap and patted her reassuringly. "I missed you, Sadie girl."

The dog moaned contentedly.

Julie eased herself onto the swing to sit on Derrick's right side. She wanted to relax with him for a while before preparing their lunch. She wanted to know why he'd been so quiet in the car.

He shifted until he could see her face. "I missed all of this." With his right hand, he gestured to include Shady Meadows. "There's no place I would rather be than here, sharing this beautiful summer day with you."

"It is a perfect day." She smiled, but her stomach growled. "Are you ready for lunch?"

"Sure, if you're hungry, I could eat."

But the intense way he was studying her indicated something other than food was on his mind. Something serious.

She cautiously rose from the swing, knowing sudden movements would jar his shoulder despite the stability afforded by the sling. She headed into the house, stopped, and made eye contact with the shepherd. "Okay, release. Sadie, come."

The dog followed her obediently.

Ten minutes later, Julie carried the pastrami on rye sandwiches, potato salad, and lemonade on her aunt's favorite silver serving tray. The shepherd bounded ahead of her, bumping open the screen door with her nose. She marched straight to Derrick and to Julie's relief did not jump up on him. The intelligent dog clearly sensed the man was recuperating, that gentle, cautious maneuvers were necessary.

At the opposite corner of the front porch, Julie set the table for their lunch. "Everything's ready," she said, then pointed to a dog bed near the door. "Sadie, lie down."

The dog nestled into the oval bed spread with a soft, red and black plaid blanket.

Derrick's brows raised in surprise. "You and Sadie have been working on quite a few new commands."

"'Off' and 'lie down' are useful commands for a man who's been injured."

Julie couldn't say 'shot.' God had protected Derrick, but she didn't want to think about his taking not one but two bullets to save her father's life. The second bullet, the one to his neck, could have easily killed him, but God had saved Derrick.

Leveling her with a quizzical look, Derrick pulled out her chair for her. "'Off' instead of 'get down' to avoid confusion with 'lie down.'"

"Exactly. You catch on fast."

"So does Sadie." Mischief twinkled in his deep blue eyes. "I guess that means we don't need any more lessons."

He was teasing her, but she refused to be distracted.

"You know how I feel about you taking Sadie home today. Since I couldn't change your mind, I needed to make sure she understood what you needed from her."

He touched Julie's cheek and leaned in to kiss her. "You're spoiling me, Jewels." He grinned. "But I don't mind being spoiled. As long as I can spoil you, too."

The determination in his sapphire eyes made her catch her breath. What did he have in mind? Dismissing her hunger, she sat in the chair he still held out for her then waited impatiently for him to sit, too.

He perched on the edge of his chair. "Before we eat, I have to ask you something important."

"Sure, of course."

He rose from his chair, pulled something from his pocket that he kept hidden in his hand, and bent down on one knee before her. "About you and me, Jewels. And our future."

She gasped. Her hands flew to her mouth, and her eyes filled with tears. He was proposing. She couldn't breathe. Couldn't say a word.

His gaze held her captive as he took her hand and placed a small velvet box in her upturned palm. "Will you marry me? Say yes and make me the happiest man in the world."

Her hand shook. She almost dropped the jewelry box. She'd been waiting for this moment from the first day Derrick and Sadie had struggled their way into her school.

He got to his feet, pulled his chair next to hers and

searched her eyes straight through to her heart. "Will you marry me? Be my wife, Jewels, and every day I'll thank God for giving me the best gift a man can have."

His sweet words stole her breath, making it impossible to speak. She bit her lower lip and nodded.

"Is that a yes?"

She wanted to leap onto his lap and throw her arms around his neck, and but she might hurt him. So, she leaned across the table and captured his face in her hands. "Of course, I'll marry you. I love you, Derrick. I will always love you."

With tears shimmering in his eyes, he cupped her chin with his right hand. His mouth met hers with a kiss infused with all the promise of their love. Her lips yielded to his, responding and offering promises of her own.

When he broke away, it took her a minute to catch her breath.

"Open the box, Jewels."

With trembling fingers, she lifted the lid to reveal a fiery diamond solitaire encircled with tiny rubies.

Derrick took the box from her hand, removed the platinum ring, and slipped it easily on her finger. It fit as though it had been made for her.

She held up her left hand in the sunlight. "This ring is the most beautiful engagement ring I've ever seen. But how did you get it to fit so perfectly?"

"Your mother helped me. My mother had larger hands than yours, so I asked your mom to borrow one of your rings, and Melanie took them both to the jeweler's for sizing."

Tears slid down Julie's face, but she ignored them. What an honor to wear his mother's engagement ring! Eager to begin making plans, she clasped Derrick's hand. "If it's okay with you, hon, I'd like an autumn wedding, maybe the weekend before Thanksgiving."

His face lit up with a light that rivaled the sun. "The sooner the better."

Epilogue

Julie studied her reflection in the full-length mirror. Her blonde hair lay in soft, obedient waves cascading over her shoulders and down her back. She'd wanted to her wear her hair up in a style more befitting a traditional bride. But Derrick preferred her hair long and loose. So, she had chosen a veil with a simple chiffon panel that covered her face in the front. The back and sides of the veil were much longer and edged in tiny silver snowflakes with shimmering rhinestones. The cuffs of the long, fitted sleeves and the V-neck of her A-line white gown were also trimmed with snowflakes adorned with sparkling rhinestone centers. Around her neck, she wore a silver pendant featuring a heart-shaped ruby. Derrick had presented it to her on Thanksgiving. As he'd placed the stunning necklace around her neck and closed the clasp, he'd whispered, "For our favorite wedding photo."

She was getting married today. In ten minutes to be exact. Where were the pre-wedding jitters she'd heard so much about? Julie had never felt more peaceful or more confident that she was exactly where God planned her to be. At exactly the right time.

She and Derrick had talked about getting married the Saturday after Thanksgiving, but her brother had complained about the inconvenience of coming home for her wedding the week before his final exams. Mom suggested they might prefer a spring wedding. Neither Derrick nor Julie were willing to wait that long.

When Melanie and Stacey spotted the perfect bridesmaid dress—a floor-length gown with an empire waist in gorgeous claret red, Julie conceded. Getting married two Saturdays before Christmas wasn't that much longer to wait. Christmas had always been her favorite time of year, and she couldn't think of a better present than waking up on Christmas morning as Mrs. Derrick Walker.

A firm knock at the door alerted her. "Honey, it's Dad."

The soft strains of the traditional wedding march sent her pulse racing. For a nanosecond, she thought she might faint. Clasping her bouquet of red Lincoln roses, white baby's breath, and Christmas greens, she breathed a quick prayer of thanks to God for this perfect day, complete with the season's first gentle snow flurries blowing outside the church windows.

She flung the door open wide for her dad, smiled up at him, and linked her arm in his.

"You look beautiful." One tear slid down his weathered cheek. "As beautiful as your mom on our wedding day."

Julie wiped the moisture from his face. "Stop. You promised not to make me cry, Dad."

"I didn't promise I wouldn't cry."

"If you cry, I'll definitely cry. Tears of joy are fine. For *after* Derrick and I say I do, but not before."

Her father schooled his features. Composed and totally in control, he smiled, took her arm, and led her to the sanctuary entrance.

They paused for a moment on the threshold of the beautifully decorated church. Red and white roses with Christmas greens adorned the altar. Swags of holly tied with red satin ribbon hung from the end of each pew. Lined up in front of the church, each member of their small wedding party smiled at Julie, excited that the moment had finally arrived. Her bridesmaids, Melanie and Stacey, were stunning in their sleek red gowns. Each woman held a single white rose tied with two silver ribbons and a single red ribbon. Leon and Jack, the best man and groomsman, wore black tuxedos with shirts matching the bridesmaids' gowns, silver bowties, and white rose boutonnieres pinned to their collars.

For a one perfect, joyous moment, Derrick caught and held her gaze. Wearing a black tuxedo with a silver dress shirt set off by claret red bowtie, and matching boutonniere, he looked so handsome she couldn't breathe. She smiled. He smiled back at her. She wanted to memorize every inch of his beloved face and the way he stood stock-still despite his obvious eagerness to sprint down the aisle and sweep her up into his arms. Which would be utterly delightful. But definitely disruptive.

Like falling dominoes, a myriad of camera flashes made her blink. So many people were taking advantage of the unexpected opportunity to photograph the bride, but she couldn't wait another minute to become Derrick's wife.

Ignoring the slow tempo of the music, she strode to the altar to meet her groom. Julie smiled as her father placed her hand in Derrick's. God's plan for her and Derrick had turned out to be more amazing than she had dared to dream, and she could hardly wait to exchange their vows.

As Pastor Steve began the wedding ceremony with "Dearly, beloved, we are gathered here today to join this man and this woman together in holy matrimony," Julie blinked back the joyful tears bubbling up from her heart. Every word, every gesture of their wedding was more wonderful than she'd imagined. She was blessed beyond measure. She wanted to sing and shout and tell everyone she was the happiest woman in the world.

As their wedding party headed down the aisle to form a receiving line in the vestibule, Derrick leaned close and whispered in her ear, "Honey, tell me what you're thinking right now?"

She lifted her face to her husband's and gazed into his incredibly blue eyes. "I'm grateful that God had a better plan for me than I had for myself. And His plan was you."

"I feel exactly the same way about you, my darling wife." He wrapped his arms around her waist, hugged her close, and kissed her cheek. "I love you, Mrs. Walker."

"I love you, too, Mr. Walker."

"Shall we?" He enclosed her hand in his and led her down the aisle to greet their friends and family and to begin their new life together.

Dear Reader,

When I began Julie and Derrick's story, I planned for this book to be a novella. But, as is often the case, God's plans are bigger than our own. I hadn't intended to publish *Love's Way Back* this year, but the Lord impressed upon my mind and heart, over the course of several months, that my readers needed a sweet, somewhat uncomplicated romance during this challenging time.

It's easy to see God's hand at work when life is moving steadily along as we expect, but when something or someone disrupts our plans or shatters our hopes, we may easily doubt God's love. But, dear reader, His plan remains the same—to give you an abundant life beyond all your hopes and dreams. Jesus has promised to never leave you nor forsake you. No matter what challenges your life may hold, my prayer is that this story has inspired you to look to God and to rely upon His unfailing love for you and for everyone dear to you. Keep your eyes and your heart open, for His boundless blessings may arrive at the most unexpected times, in the most unexpected ways.

I would be happy to hear from you. Please contact me at authorlaurahervey@gmail.com.

Yours truly,

Laura Hervey

If you enjoyed this book, please consider giving me a review on Amazon, Goodreads, or your favorite book review site.

About Laura Hervey

Laura Hervey writes inspirational romance. Her first novel, *Scarlet Tears,* is a redemption story about a former call girl who seeks to rebuild her life. Her second redemption novel, *Light in a Dark Place,* tells the story of two young people whose love is tested by drug addiction and an unplanned pregnancy. Laura is also the author of a variety of short works, including articles, opinion pieces, poetry, short stories, and devotionals.

Laura lives in Western New York. She attends the Bible Tabernacle, a non-denominational Christian church and is a member of American Christian Fiction Writers. She teaches 9th grade English at her alma mater. When she isn't writing or teaching, she enjoys spending time with her two children, their spouses, and her grandchildren. She shares her home with two dogs, a German shepherd named Lacey Marie and a miniature Dachshund called Deenie.

Follow Laura on Facebook @AuthorLauraHervey, on Twitter @AuthorHervey, and on Instagram @laurafhervey. You may also visit Laura at her author website, www.laurahervey.com.

Also available from Amazon:

Scarlet Tears
Can a former call girl accept God's redemptive grace?
http://www.amazon.com/dp/B07FMNJ84L/

Light in a Dark Place
Can Luke and Abby find God's grace and accept that sometimes reality demands new dreams?
http://www.amazon.com/dp/B07XXJJQVW/